# DARKNESS FALLING

HELENA DAHLGREN

TRANSLATION BY
TARA CHACE

Andrews McMeel
PUBLISHING®

NORTHSHIRE

The Great
Reservoir

CRATER OF ICE

Ashland

Valley of the
Hidden Dinosaur

CENTRAL JORVIK

Firgrove
Village

GROVE

Jorvik City

MISTFALL

uth Link

Dundull

RN JORVIK

Other *Soul Riders* books
by Helena Dahlgren

*Jorvik Calling*
*The Legend Awakens*

To my readers, a constant source of encouragement even when the going gets tough (and sometimes it does, not just for the Soul Riders).

I'm sure all authors think that THEIR readers in particular are the best readers in the world. In my case this just happens to be true.

When I think of you, it just makes me happy. Thank you!

*"Good friends are like stars. You can't always see them—but you know they're always there."*

—Anon

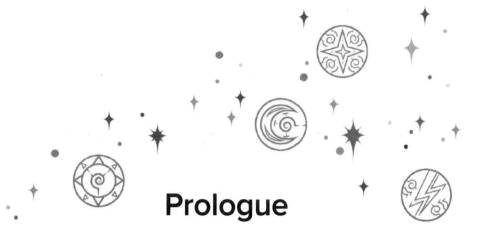

# Prologue

Sometimes people say, "It must grow dark before it can become light again," but what does that really mean? Could it mean that the really challenging parts of life are necessary in order for hope to return—and with it, light? Or is it just something we say to comfort ourselves when our lives feel tough?

When darkness falls over the earth, giving up feels easy. What if it's already too late to do anything about it? On an island called Jorvik, four girls take fate into their own hands. They're doing something about it.

They are the last Soul Riders, and this is the story of their first big battle against evil.

*"Don't you understand? We caused this!"*

The words rang in their ears as they galloped across Jorvik's desolate plains, the horses kicking up clods of dirt in their wake. Beyond the field where no flowers grow, at least not this late in the fall, a big, black raven rose from a tree. It emitted a guttural caw as it flew away.

The four chosen ones watched in silence as the bird rose into the sky. They had hardly spoken a word to each other since they left the Secret Stone Circle. There was no need.

What was left to say? As they stood there among the rune-stones, absorbing just how bad the situation really was, Linda had said what everyone else was thinking.

*It was us. We're the ones who did this. We rushed it. We were too impatient, and now all of Jorvik will pay the price.*

When they teleported themselves back to the Secret Stone Circle, a strong, rare magic was released, affecting the nature of the island. Now that magic was about to cause a disaster, and it was all their fault.

Because of them, the large Bastion Dam, the one preventing Winter Valley from flooding with water, was on the verge of bursting, putting an entire village in danger. This was hard to accept, especially considering the fact that there was a chance that they would fail, but they were heading to the dam now in hopes of making things right.

Lisa took the lead on her horse, Starshine. Even though the sky was a dismal gray, like the color of dull, old pencil lead, Starshine's coat gleamed white. His glorious blue mane and tail shimmered under the heavy cloud cover. Even now, when everything around them had turned into chaos and they were under so much pressure that she thought she might break, Lisa was grateful for her horse, grateful that it was the two of them to the end.

She shortened the reins and closed her eyes, shutting out the world for a moment. Her red hair danced in a gust of gathering wind. *This has all happened so fast,* she thought. Not that long ago, she was just Lisa Peterson. Now she was a Soul Rider. Would her life ever return to normal? Was there even such a thing as normal anymore?

She closed her eyes tighter, feeling the rustle of the wind. Sometimes it felt like everything that had happened to them was just a fairy tale, but not a pleasant, warm fairy tale. Sure, there was plenty of happiness, friendship, and kindness in the story, but there were also other, darker things. Far too many other things that threatened to extinguish the light.

With her cold hands pressed into Starshine's warm mane, she thought about how it had all started. It really wasn't that long ago at all.

## 2

It had all started when Lisa and her father arrived in Jorvik a few weeks into the fall semester. Of course, it had really started long, long before that. The girls just hadn't been aware of it. The legend of the Soul Riders was already written into the island's rich soil, into the ocean's whitecaps, into Goldenhills Valley, where the fall leaves crunched and blazed vivid colors all year round. The sleeping legend was there within Jorvik's special horses, the Starbreeds, which weren't found anywhere else in the world, and it was there at the Secret Stone Circle, of course. There, high up in the mountains, the druids had helped new Soul Riders find and refine their powers for generations. The druids were wise men and women with close ties to nature. They were a natural part of Jorvik, if you knew where to look.

The Soul Riders were four young girls with magical powers. When they stood united, together with their Starbreeds, those powers were brought to life. The Soul Riders' job was to protect the delicate balance between good and evil so that Jorvik could continue to be the very special, magical place that it was.

But over the millennia, an evil force had been at work to do all it could to disrupt that balance of power, and that evil had a name: Garnok. Old ghost stories told of fishermen who had been shipwrecked at sea and devoured—not by the powerful waves, but by a fiendish beast who lured them to the bottom of the ocean. It was said that he could control minds, that once you sensed his presence you would never be yourself again. Garnok was still there, still being held captive just outside of our world. The island's forces for good sought to ensure that he never managed to escape, while the forces for evil sought to free him from his captivity.

The evil forces were led by a man named John Sands, the owner of the mysterious company Dark Core, who had been poisoned for several hundred years by the dark influence and promises of Garnok. Together, these forces wanted to release the dark magic and share in Garnok's power, while Mr. Sands also dreamed of getting revenge on the people of Jorvik for everything that had been taken from him so long ago.

The Soul Riders' horses possessed a powerful magic, and in the wrong hands that magic could be used to release Garnok once and for all. That was why Mr. Sands had kidnapped Lisa's horse, Starshine, and sent Anne's horse, Concorde, to Pandoria, a warped, nightmare-like parallel world where thoughts became fragile and everything pulsated pink.

It was all so new. It really hadn't been that long since the four Soul Riders had first come together. As they started to understand their mission, they grasped that this wasn't the kind of job they could just turn down. They were Soul Riders, regardless of how they felt about the matter, and they had to work together if they were going to succeed.

Yes, it was all so new, but they had already accomplished more than they could have ever dreamed of. They had succeeded in rescuing Starshine and Concorde, and they had convinced the witch Pi, who dwelled in a swamp deep in Goldenhills Valley, to give them the Light Ceremony book. They had managed to shake off the Dark Riders—Sabine, Jessica, and Katja—who had chased them in the woods. And most importantly: they had reunited. Because the Soul Riders had to be together; they understood that now. Together, with their horses, they were at their strongest, just as Elizabeth, their beloved friend and mentor, had said.

But the Soul Riders had already faced a heavy loss. Calliope, Elizabeth's horse, had drowned in Pi's swamp. Lisa could still hear the terrible sounds from that fateful day. They echoed inside her, the shrill shrieks that had slowly subsided until the only sounds remaining were sobs of grief.

As they tried to escape from Cauldron Swamp, the witch Pi had transformed Elizabeth—the friendly wise druid who had taught the girls so much about the Soul Riders' mission and the wisdom of the Keepers of Aideen—into a will-o'-the-wisp. She still remained in the same fluttering, flickering form, waiting for someone to change her back. She couldn't comfort the girls and tell them that everything would be okay. She couldn't take the lead, riding off on her beautiful, dapple-gray Calliope.

The Soul Riders had experienced both success and loss in the brief time that they had known each other. Now, all of their focus was on saving the dam and preventing this disaster. They had to keep the dam from breaking like it had time and time again in Linda's awful visions.

But the dam wasn't their only problem. Lisa and the others were slowly starting to realize that something more was happening on Jorvik. A darkness was gathering. The island itself was in jeopardy, and saving the dam was only a small part of the threat that the Soul Riders were facing.

Lisa was having a hard time focusing on their mission at the dam. She was having a hard time focusing on anything at all, actually. She was too distracted by the most important thing of all: her father, Carl, who was being held prisoner inside Dark

Core's headquarters. He had been captured by Mr. Sands and his henchmen, the Dark Riders. For a brief moment, Lisa had been Mr. Sands's prisoner herself, and she knew that he was prepared to do whatever it took to get his way. He might torture her father, or possibly even kill him. What was a dam crisis compared to the threat of losing the only parent you had left?

*Don't think like that,* she told herself. *First the dam, then Dad. It has to be that way.*

Yes—it had to be that way, but that didn't mean that it had to feel right.

Lisa opened her eyes and sat up straight in the saddle. She felt the impatience crawling under her skin and blistering there.

"Hurry up!" Lisa called to the others, urging Starshine along. "Come on, you guys!"

The other riders picked up their pace and they all galloped onward in the direction of the dam. Starshine puffed out his nostrils and shook his head back and forth. It was almost as if he was trying to warn her about something. Lisa shook her head in an effort to force away the thought. They didn't have time for that now.

**3**

They rode on at high speed. The fall air was chilly, but none of them were cold anymore. Their faces looked determined. In the pale gray light, the four young girls galloped side by side, just as the old stories had foretold. Linda, Lisa, Alex, and Anne rode together just as they had so many times before.

And yet something was different this time. *Everything* was different. The river ran through Winter Valley just like it always had, but the water level was so high that big, wet pools of mud had formed along the riverbank. The horses' hooves squelched as they neared the river. They were forced to slow down to keep from slipping.

"Is it going to be like this the rest of the way?" Anne asked, making a face.

Linda shortened her reins and shook her head.

"We just have to move farther away from the river," she said. "Then we'll be able to gallop on firmer ground again."

She hoped that what she said was true. They didn't have time to do this at the leisurely pace of a walk or trot. They really needed to be able to gallop now. She gave a deep sigh of relief when they moved farther away from the riverbank and the ground stopped squelching. The water wasn't a problem anymore, not for the moment at least. Linda straightened up in her saddle and let Meteor choose how quickly he wanted to gallop. Strong, sensible Meteor. A wave of gratitude flowed through her as she thought about how perfectly they understood each other, how she barely had to give him cues in order for him to understand what she wanted. Where would she be without him?

They heard the sound of thundering hooves in the woods behind them as a herd of wild horses fled in panic. The Soul Riders' horses heard the wild horses fleeing and seemed ready to bolt themselves. Their eyes bulged and their muscles tensed beneath their sweaty coats. There would be no slowing them down now, even if the girls had wanted to. People say that animals can sense when something terrible is about to happen, that they have a kind of sixth sense that allows them to pick up on impending danger long before humans can.

The girls had been riding with a sense of dread in their stomachs the whole time, but when they heard the wild horses panicking, that feeling of dread dissolved, turning into sheer, wild desperation. The animals knew that the rising water level in the river wasn't coming from the rain.

All magic has consequences. The girls knew that now, far too well. The awful words that no one wanted to say echoed through the empty space between them, rising up into the gray, rain-laden sky. Maybe the words were in the blackbird's song—was that why it sang out so mournfully?

*It was us. We caused this.*

Linda already knew how it was going to happen. She had seen it play out in her visions too many times to count. At first, she hadn't understood what she was seeing. It was impossible to sort the images, to see how they were connected. For a while, it was all just dark water and muffled cries, a heavy pressure on her chest that made it hard to breathe. But now she knew what it all meant, and that icy certainty made her press her hands firmly into Meteor's thick, rough mane for comfort. She felt his warmth underneath her hands, as well as how fast he was breathing. A small part of her wanted to disappear into this moment. Into a *before* that far too soon would turn into an *after*. She didn't want to think about what would follow. As long as they were still riding, as long as they were on their way there, they might be able to prevent this disaster. As long as they continued to ride, she dared to hope.

In spite of everything.

When it happened—if it happened—the water would race straight down the valley toward the houses in the village below. There would be tremendous devastation. Linda sat up straighter in her saddle. She let the rhythm of Meteor's gallop wash away all of the haunting echoes of panicked horses, terrified parents, children crying for their mothers, that awful gurgling before everything went silent. The silence might actually be the worst of all.

Linda blinked several times in an effort to clear the terrible images from her mind. Then she turned to Alex, who was riding closest to her. "We need to warn them, make sure that they get out of their houses—all the people living along the river below the dam, I mean. If . . . if this doesn't work, they can't be there when the dam breaks."

Alex nodded grimly and urged Tin-Can on. On the other side of her, Anne did the same.

"This *has* to work!" Lisa half-whispered. Linda caught her eye and gave her friend an encouraging smile.

"Almost showtime," Linda said.

"Argh, we've hardly had any chance to rehearse," Alex mumbled. And then in a louder voice, she said, "I think the druids should have come with us. Are we sure we can do this ourselves?"

"You know very well that we didn't have time to wait for the druids," Linda said, shaking her head impatiently. "They're not exactly the fastest-moving bunch, and we didn't have a second to waste." She was quiet for a moment, brushing away a dark strand of hair that had come loose from her thick bun. Then she continued. "I mean, after all, this isn't *that* tricky! We've got this. All we need to do is stop the magical cracks from growing, and then shrink them using the magic of the Light Ceremony. And we have everything we need right here."

She gently patted her saddlebag that contained the Light Ceremony book. For centuries and centuries, the book had helped to guide young Soul Riders in Jorvik. Now, it was their turn.

Linda suddenly had a flashback to the time when she was at the local swimming pool and had to jump off of the ten-meter diving platform. It was several years ago, and her parents were still living in Jorvik. She could remember it all so clearly, that tickling sensation in her stomach, the way she held her breath in fear. Everything had just stopped as the diving platform seemed to give way beneath her. All other sounds disappeared until all she could hear was the intense pounding of her heart.

*Thump, thump, thump.*

And then when she finally jumped: butterflies had spread throughout her entire body. She had done it!

She felt like being a Soul Rider was a little like standing up there on that diving platform and daring to jump into the water below. Except for the fact that as a Soul Rider, you had to be prepared to dive in over and over again and there was no guarantee that there would be any water to soften your landing.

Alex looked at Linda. Her friend's eyes glowed behind her fogged-up glasses and Alex couldn't help but feel some of her confidence.

"Okay," Alex replied, picking up the pace of her gallop. "Here we go!"

# 4

It felt good to ride side by side for as long as they could. The wide field would soon give way to narrow forest trails winding all the way to the dam. But first, they had to ride to the valley below and try to warn the people of the village that stood in the water's path. They planned to knock on as many doors as they could, hoping that someone would take their warning seriously.

Across the field, in the shade of the surrounding trees and mountains, they saw a little red house. Outside of the house, there was a small green yard with a trampoline, and a gravel driveway with two cars in it. They slowed down, first to a trot and then to a walk as they rode toward the house. *What a beautiful place to live,* Lisa thought, *secluded and peaceful.* Her gaze swept over the porch, which was already decorated for Halloween. A plastic skull danced cheerfully in the wind. She shivered, wishing that she had taken the time to put on her fleece jacket before setting out. The cold was seeping into her skin now like ice water. The reality of the situation was sinking in even deeper as she scanned the property.

If the dam broke, then the water would overtake them and carry everything away with it. It would carry away all the people who lived down here.

A small child, maybe three years old, rushed out the open front door with a toy horse in his hand. He caught sight of the girls and their horses and squealed in delight. Lisa waved to him. Then she rode forward and said hello, then asked, "Are your parents at home?"

The boy didn't have a chance to answer before a man in jeans and a T-shirt stepped out onto the small porch and smiled hesitantly at them. His smile quickly faded when he saw the looks on their faces. He picked the child up, his eyes moving between the four young riders.

"Has something happened?"

"The dam," the girls responded in unison. Then Linda clarified, "We think it's going to collapse! Please, you have to evacuate the village! Now!"

The man stood there on his porch holding his child. He stared at them for a second before he responded. "If this is joke, then it's not very funny."

"Believe me, I wish it was a joke," Alex said. "But we're serious. Please, we don't have time to explain more right now, just evacuate the area. Leave right away, and warn your neighbors, too. Please!"

This time the man did not respond. Instead, he stood there rocking back and forth a bit. The boy made a fuss and wriggled out of his father's arms. He started to play with his plastic horse on the porch, dragging the hooves of the toy along the wooden railing. The father remained silent, his forehead wrinkled and his eyes focusing first on Alex and then Linda, Anne, and Lisa—and then on Alex again. The little boy tugged impatiently at his arm.

"Come on, Dad! The car! Quick! Krikelin doesn't like the water." He gestured toward his toy horse.

"We're not going anywhere," the father said emphatically. "I'm not getting in the car just because some strange girls on horseback told me to."

Linda felt a surge of anger and frustration well up inside her. She swallowed hard before she said, in a voice that sounded calmer than she felt, "I know how this sounds, but we're serious. I've had visions," she continued. "I've seen things." In her mind, she saw a plastic horse figurine being washed away in a massive wave. And she saw a pudgy, fumbling child's hand eventually becoming terribly still. Then she blinked hard.

"If what we think is going to happen happens . . ."

She waited until the man looked at her again.

"If what we think is going to happen happens," she repeated in the same calm, steady voice as before, "then it's going to turn out really badly. Please, evacuate the area! For your son's sake. You've seen the water level of the river rising with your own eyes."

"Hey, don't get my son mixed up in your foolishness," he responded harshly. "It's normal for the water level to rise in the fall when the rains come. I've lived along this river my whole life. I know what I'm talking about—unlike you, I might add."

Alex felt the necklace she always wore—the one shaped like a bolt of lightning—burning at the base of her throat, like fire. She clenched her fists in her pockets and thought of all the things she wanted to say to the man standing before them. The angry words and insults stuck in her throat. But Linda gave her a look of warning.

*Do not give him any more ammunition to use against us right now,* Linda's look said. *He already thinks we're crazy.*

So, Alex bit her tongue, but the lightning bolt continued to burn at her throat. She glared angrily at the man, hoping that she might accidentally shoot off a mini-bolt with her eyes so that he would realize his mistake. But he just laughed. He laughed right in her face.

"So, you think we rode all the way out here just to play a *trick* on you?!" Alex hissed, unable to remain quiet any longer. "Like we don't have anything better to do? Listen to what we're telling you! The dam is going to break, and when that happens ... believe me, you don't want to be here."

The man had stopped laughing. He turned around toward his half-open front door so that he had his back to them.

"I'm going to have to ask you to leave now," he said. "You're scaring my son. Don't you see that? But you're welcome to come back on Halloween. You can choose a trick or a treat, but I'm pretty sure I already know which one you're going to pick."

Alex opened her mouth to respond, but Anne shook her head.

"There's no point, Alex. We've done what we can. Let's hurry up to the dam and try to stop it from collapsing. We still have a chance."

"But we have to warn the other villagers, don't we?" Alex said, but she swallowed hard when her eyes met Anne's. She understood. No one was going to believe them, four young girls. And there was no time to argue with people who refused to listen. They had to get to the dam before it was too late.

The little boy raised his plastic horse to say goodbye as they rode away. For a brief moment, Lisa looked into the little boy's eyes and saw someone else in there. A little girl with her red hair standing straight up and a shimmering white model horse grasped firmly in her hand, sticky from candy.

When the grown-ups asked her what the horse's name was, she always shrugged because she didn't really know. But now she knew that his name was Starshine.

Lisa looked away from the child and rode to catch up with her friends. She was just about to break into a trot when she heard a childlike yell.

"Wait!" It was the little boy, who had run down from his porch and out into the yard. He ran after them, clutching his toy horse. "Krikelin can't swim," he said, looking at her wide-eyed. "He's going to drown."

Lisa looked the child right in the eye and hoped that he wouldn't notice her eyes starting to fill with tears.

"Krikelin isn't going to drown," she said firmly. "My friends and I, we're going to stop this bad thing from happening. I promise, we'll do everything we can."

It hurt her to see the boy light up. *Don't make promises you can't keep,* she thought, and remembered all the times that some older person had told her that everything was going to work out. And then everything didn't work out. Lisa knew what it felt like to be promised things that would never happen. And still the words came, falsely comforting, running out of her mouth like water.

"I promise," she said. "Don't be scared."

Alex gave Lisa a long look and shook her head. Her golden-brown eyes, which always reminded Lisa of the old-fashioned caramels she used to buy at the candy store when she was little, looked almost black against the quickly darkening clouds. Lisa looked at the boy one last time. Then she let Starshine break into a trot. And then they were on their way, the final leg of the journey to the dam, hearts beating so hard in their chests that it felt like they would leap right out. Their heartbeats nearly drowned out the tremendous noise of the rushing water that was getting closer and closer as they neared the dam.

*Please,* Lisa thought, leaning her cheek against Starshine's neck. *Let us make it in time.*

# 5

The narrow, winding path led them higher and higher. They walked slowly; every step among the uneven stones was an effort for the horses. The horses' bodies were steaming from their journey in the chilly mountain air. Everything looked so small when they glanced back down at the village, like Legos. Linda's eyes glazed over as they panned over the tiny red and white houses below. She squinted in an effort to see if there were still two cars parked in front of the house they had visited earlier, but they were too far away now.

Linda's visions were excruciatingly strong now. She barely had time to breathe before a new gruesome image—hardly more than a flicker, a movie that was over before it had a chance to begin—grabbed her mind, clinging like a cold, clammy hand.

And now the people had faces. Now, she knew whose little hand it was. She knew who was going to disappear into the dark, turbulent water when the dam broke.

She heard screaming and crying. *"Krikelin can't swim!"*

She watched everything get washed away as the dam burst.

A barbecue apron that said "World's Best Dad" on it.

The jack-o'-lantern smashed into a thousand pieces as the water flooded the porch. The skeleton that continued his dance of death in the floodwaters.

A big hand that grabbed hold of the little lifeless body.

The tears that would never end.

All the wreckage, all the debris, that had recently been someone's life.

No. *No.* It can't happen! Linda clutched her saddle until her knuckles turned white, urging quiet thoughts into her mind. Then, finally, she managed to stave off the visions. She smiled weakly as she saw an almost invisible sliver of moon glimmering in the heavy gray sky. It quickly disappeared behind a cloud, but just knowing that it was there calmed her pulse. She sat up straight in the saddle and hoped that the last little bit of the ride wouldn't be too difficult. The horses were tired now, she knew that. But what choice did they have? They couldn't stop now. They had to keep going.

So, they kept going. The farther up they got, the harder it was to progress forward. The trail was full of twists and turns and bordered by tall pine trees and moss-covered boulders. There were puddles here and there that got bigger as the trail grew smaller and steeper. Concorde scraped the ground with his hooves to get rid of the water.

Anne cautiously looked down. She scanned the wet ground, searching for footprints, some kind of indication that someone had been there before them. Nothing. No one had ridden there for some time.

The noise of the raging water was so loud now that it roared in their ears.

"Do you guys hear that?" she yelled to the others. "It's not far now."

"How could we NOT hear that?" Lisa replied, scanning up toward the summit where she could see something big and shimmering silver among the pine trees and the tall piles of stone.

The roar of the water worried her. Was it really supposed to be this noisy? What if . . . what if it had already happened? She gulped, trying to shake those thoughts, cold and slippery as the rocks under Starshine's frantically struggling hooves.

*No point in getting ahead of ourselves,* she thought. *We'll know soon.*

No one said very much during the very last leg of the trip. The tremendous roar of the water drowned out all words, so there was barely any point in trying to talk. But their minds were racing. Some of their thoughts were clear, others so vague that there were hardly words to describe them, just feelings.

Anne stretched in her saddle. Her legs and abdominal muscles were sore from the long ride. Her eyes were full of tears from the wind. Now, when they were almost there, she finally dared to unleash her anxiety. It felt good to do that. Somehow, she felt calmer for acknowledging to herself how hard this all felt.

*This will never work. But I don't dare say that out loud, of course. No need to create mass panic, right? Although, in all honestly, I do not see how this can work. We're completely in over our heads. Sorry, but it's true. Don't the others get that? Linda, for example. She seems so sure, but I wonder . . .*

Anne glanced back at Linda, who was riding behind her. She was riding in a forward seat to relieve the pressure on Meteor, who was loyally walking along at a steady pace.

Linda's keen eye constantly scanned ahead and back—but in her mind, she was losing ground. She tried to focus, even though her thoughts were swirling around like crazy.

*It's all happening so fast. I can't keep up. Can't we just hold on for a minute and try to see what's what? Maybe if I just tried to analyze one thing at a time . . .*

She took a deep breath, and then she thought of the Light Ceremony and the powerful book that she had in her saddlebag, the one that was going to guide them. Books had helped her countless times before, carried her through periods of loneliness and fear. Linda's world had opened up under the glow of her reading lamp, become so much bigger and more magical than she had ever dared to hope. Now, she felt the shimmering magic of the Light Ceremony book. She trembled as she thought about how important the book was. People had literally died to access its magic. Now it was theirs.

*It's just a book—an ancient, magical book, but still . . . a book. We can do this. I mean, what choice do we have? Exactly. We have no choice. Fine. Okay, the Light Ceremony. What does it involve? If you boil it down? Something about a seal, right? Exactly: create a light seal and seal the cracks. Light is stronger than darkness. But . . . is that really true? The worst thing is that all the others probably think that I have a plan. Do I have a plan? I don't know . . . what would Hermione do? Ugh, forget about her right now. Maybe right now it's more relevant to ask: what would Alex do?*

Linda turned around and met Alex's resolute look. She couldn't guess what Alex was thinking. Alex could be every bit as harsh and impenetrable as the smooth, slippery stones on the ground below them. But by this time, Linda knew that Alex often said exactly what she was thinking. Or at least, what needed to be said. Linda kept looking at Alex until her friend raised her eyebrows as if to say, *what?* Alex opened her mouth and said something to Linda, but her voice was drowned out by the increasing sound of the water. With a dejected look, Alex turned her thoughts inward instead, while Tin-Can hurried along.

*It is so incredibly frustrating not to be able to talk to the others right now because of all this noise. I'm going to go nuts from being alone with my thoughts. Plus, I can't stop thinking about that father down there in the village. He just laughed at us. Why does it feel like no one takes us seriously?*

Behind her, a loud whinny penetrated the roar of the water. Alex glanced back over her shoulder and saw Lisa trying to calm Starshine. Her face was totally white and her eyes moist.

*Lisa looks so frail,* Alex thought, *as if she might fall apart any minute. Do I look like that, too? I hope she holds it together now. I hope we ALL hold it together, because to be totally honest, I can't bear to think of the alternative . . .*

Lisa managed to calm Starshine by humming a song. Now she was struggling with the tears welling up in her eyes as thoughts of her father settled over her like a thick veil.

*I wonder how he is. How could I agree to ride here instead of going off to save him?! Especially after Mr. Sands admitted that he was holding him captive. I must be the worst daughter in the world. Please, hang on, Dad. I'm coming soon . . . but first, the dam. Linda's probably right that we can do this. Somehow. Together. But it is so freaking cold and lonely and I feel like a four-year-old who's lost my stuffed horsey . . . besides, weren't the druids a little bit quick to send us here? Why didn't any of them offer to come with us? I've got a bad feeling about this. What if they're prepared to sacrifice us . . . ? How do we know we can trust them? For real? I mean, we hardly know them. I wish Elizabeth could tell us what to do. Oh, Elizabeth . . .*

The water was squelching and splashing around the horses' legs now. Meteor flinched and flattened his ears. Linda knew that her horse wasn't afraid of the water. They had flown effortlessly over countless water hazards in competitions. The last time he reacted to water like this was when . . .

But no. She didn't want to think about that.

She couldn't stop herself, though.

*When I was at Pine Hill Mansion and I left Meteor outside, he carried on like this, as if something or someone was waiting for him as soon as I was out of the picture . . . Sabine and Khaan. What if they beat us here? And Jessica and Katja, too? They certainly took a bad fall from the bridge, but they seem to be able to cope with almost anything. What if they're up there, just waiting? And we're walking right into their trap . . . like naive little lambs.*

She stopped herself in mid-thought. Because ahead of them, just beyond the final peak, the big, shiny silver object had risen from the mist. Now they could see that it was a building. A fort, maybe, or an old church. Or something in between. There were vaults and arches, thick walls, niches, and bay windows. Different sections, some really old, others newer, forming a vast, mighty whole. Mist from the waterfall rose up in front of the gigantic stone body. The tremendous force of the water made them feel small, inconsequential.

One by one they slid off their horses and stared up at the imposing sight.

They had made it to the dam.

# 6

Some places in Jorvik existed in obscurity. They were there, but no one thought about them very much. The big dam, which controlled the island's water flow and provided extra irrigation during the dry summer months, was just such a place. Many people lived their entire lives on the island without ever visiting the large dam. Why would someone bother to come all the way out there, beyond civilization, when there were so many other wonderful things in Jorvik to discover?

But anyone who did make the effort to come here would certainly never forget the place.

"Wow!" Alex exclaimed. "I didn't even know this place existed."

Everyone looked up at the enormous stone building that towered in front of the dam. It appeared both massive and dignified at the same time. Even in the muted gray afternoon light, the facade gleamed of silver and gold. The water in the reservoir stretched out behind it, but beyond that they could just make out the blue-tinged mountain peaks and a milky white sky with black around the edges. They led the horses past the fort-like building, following the narrow, winding paths. Soon, they stood completely still, gazing out at the aqueducts and pools that were part of the structure of the dam.

"Are you sure this is a reservoir and not a lake or an ocean?" Lisa yelled.

When she had heard the place described, it had somehow sounded small, she thought. But the actual body of water spreading out in front of them was anything but small.

A strong pink light shone from the dam structure, expanding gradually like a climbing vine. A lump formed in the pit of Anne's stomach when she saw that light. Because that meant that the Pandorian cracks were already so big that they had begun to spread, slowly opening up and threatening to expose our world to the other world of Pandoria.

And then there was the water, of course, the massive reservoir filled to the brim with sparkling blue water that had already started to overflow. Everyone peered around anxiously. None of them could know for sure because they hadn't ever been here before, but was there really supposed to be *so* much water?

Tin-Can stamped his hooves in a big puddle and whinnied shrilly.

"There, there," Alex said, stroking his long, tangled mane. "It's just a little water. For the moment, anyway," she added darkly.

Lisa's cheeks grew pale, but then she turned around toward the building, which was hard to keep her eyes off of.

"What kind of place is this?" Lisa wondered.

"A school for wizards?" Anne suggested dryly.

If Linda were herself right now, she would surely have added that, yes, as a matter of fact a long, long time ago, Bastion Dam, which towered over the Great Reservoir, had once been a popular gathering place for those interested in magic and sorcery. People believed that the water here had magical properties. Alchemists traveled there in pursuit of gold, and strange experiments were conducted deep below the water's surface. No one knew exactly *what* people had been searching for. An underwater city perhaps, some thought. Others whispered of mermaids and water creatures. Then one day the pilgrimages ceased, and the residents of the island transformed it into what would become Jorvik's primary source of water and electricity today.

But Linda didn't say any of that. She remained fearfully silent as her friends chattered on. She was relieved not to be alone with her thoughts anymore, and grateful to be able to pretend that everything was okay for just a little while longer. As long as no one said it out loud, they could try to pretend that this was a totally normal riding outing. Linda wondered, should she break that illusion now?

*Time to stop pretending.*

"We've been riding for a long time," Linda said. "I don't know how you guys feel, but I'm totally exhausted. And the visions I keep having aren't exactly helping things. Please, I just need a few minutes to pull myself together. Then we'll begin the ceremony."

The others nodded and sighed in relief. *Thank you*, Lisa thought, smiling at Linda. Anne walked over to her saddlebag and took out apples and water for the horses. As always, their chewing noises had a calming effect on her. Everything was quiet for a while. They waited for Linda. Her voice was dark and hoarse when she finally said, "*If* the dam breaks. Then it will only be after we've done everything we can, absolutely everything in our power, to stop it."

Linda gently patted the book in her saddlebag. It felt like magic, like saying *knock on wood* for good luck.

Alex nodded slowly. "Yes," she said, her voice trembling slightly. "Everything. And the book will help us. Linda, isn't it time to get it out now and get started?"

Everyone stared as Linda pulled the Light Ceremony book out of the saddlebag. The cover's gold foiling shimmered and emitted glowing reflections that bounced off the dam. Anne inhaled deeply and so did Linda.

"I can't believe the druids let us ride off on our own with this book," Anne said, gazing at the cover as if enthralled.

"I can," Lisa mumbled. When the others stared at her blankly, she shook herself angrily. "I mean, I'm sorry, you guys, but surely you've had the same thought?"

"What thought?" Linda asked, rubbing her head. She wasn't feeling as clear-headed as usual and it was bothering her.

"Honestly," Lisa responded. "What have the druids done to help us? Am I the only one who gets the feeling that they *wanted* to send us here on our own with the book?" She paused for a moment, putting her hand on Starshine's slender neck. "You know," she continued slowly, "that if anything happens . . . then they can then blame it on us. That's pretty convenient, right?"

Anne felt a strange twinge. She suddenly remembered something that Elizabeth had told her before the others arrived at the Stone Circle.

Elizabeth had also been a Soul Rider—in the Sun Circle, just like Anne. Before Elizabeth had been transformed into a will-o'-the-wisp by the witch Pi, she had told Anne about her time as a Soul Rider. Not that they really had a lot of time to talk about many details that day, but . . .

"Elizabeth said something about a sisterhood that was broken," she told the others. "When she was a Soul Rider. But . . . what if that's just the druids' version of what happened? Maybe they'll say the same thing about us afterward, after the dam breaks and we've failed?"

Lisa's big eyes darkened. Her voice sounded scornful as she said, *"Elizabeth and her sisterhood, they weren't ready. All of the signs were there, but they turned out not to be right. The sisterhood was broken.*

We might as well accept it—we're replaceable, just like the Soul Riders that came before us."

"Surely you don't mean that, Lisa. Do you?" Alex said, shaking her head vigorously. "The druids are our friends! They would never lie to us."

"Honestly, Alex," Lisa scoffed. "Do you actually believe that? Don't you remember how that father down in the village looked at us when we told him about the dam? What makes you think the druids are so different? What's the deal with you constantly defending the druids, anyway? That's not like you."

Alex rolled her eyes.

"Uh, maybe because they have actually *helped* us, Lisa!" Alex exclaimed. "The Secret Stone Circle, the Soul Rider training, legends, any of that ringing any bells? The druids are basically the only ones who believe in us."

"So far," Lisa replied. "I'm sorry, but right now we can't rely on any grown-ups. All we have is each other. And our horses. These are the only things we can really be certain of."

"I wish Elizabeth were here," Alex sighed.

Lisa nodded sadly. She thought to herself, *And I wish my father was here and could take me far away from here. I wish that I had never found out that I'm a Soul Rider.*

"We all wish that," Anne said. "But Elizabeth isn't here now, so we have no choice but to handle this by ourselves." Then she straightened up so much so that Linda thought she looked almost queen-like.

She took a firmer hold of the Light Ceremony book. She felt the light continuing to dance and flow from the cover. The aged leather cover was warm against her hand. "All for the sisterhood," she said and reached for Alex's hand. "The sisterhood will be victorious. It will be so. No more broken sisterhoods, no breaking of dams. You guys, I know that we are all super scared right now. I wish I could say that everything will be fine, that I have an amazing plan, but the truth is?" She laughed, a dark, joyless laugh that sounded more like a snort. "The truth is that I'm completely lost. I don't know how we're going to fix this. But I do know one thing. We're strong together. And together we will figure this out."

Lisa wiped a tear from her cheek. Then she nodded. Alex nodded, too. Her eyes had brightened. That Alex twinkle was back.

The horses nodded emphatically by shaking their heads up and down. Then they snorted loudly, one by one, scattering warm, slimy saliva through the chilly air. Anne got splashed in the face and wiped it away with a crooked smile.

"Was that a yes, Concorde?" she said, rubbing his muzzle. He gave her a warm, gentle look as if he wanted to say, *We've got this, Anne. Together.*

Then she looked away, and what she saw made all the cozy equine warmth drain from her body. Suddenly she was shivering from the cold and she couldn't get a word out.

"Anne . . . ?" Linda said, turning toward her. "Are you okay?"

But Anne didn't respond. She just stared at the stone wall surrounding the reservoir as if she were under a spell.

"Anne?" Linda repeated. "What is it?"

Slowly, as if in a trance, Anne pointed to a deep crack in the wall. A bright, pink light glowed around the crack. The pink light pulsed faster and faster before a loud crunching sound made them all jump. Anne's trembling index finger pointed as she tried to show them what she saw.

The others saw it too now, but, oh, how they wish they hadn't.

Strange, shadow-like creatures crawled out of the crack, one by one. Writhing, hissing, and twisting, they moved deeper into the water. Where they swam, the water turned a brilliant pink.

Their red eyes gleamed.

Lisa gasped. "What *are* those?" she whispered.

Anne felt an icy sensation creeping over her body. She had hoped that she would never have to feel this way again. She had thought that this sensation belonged to another world.

"They're shadow seekers," she whispered. "From Pandoria. What are they doing here?"

# 7

The shadow seekers were everywhere. Scrambling and scratching, they crawled ever closer over the slippery rocks around the edges of the reservoir. Alex flung out her hand and tried to shoot off a lightning bolt, but it just bounced off the wall of the dam behind a writhing shadow seeker. Then, the lightning sputtered into the water with a faint sizzle. Alex felt deflated inside when she realized that her lightning wasn't enough to stop the shadow seekers. She tried again and missed. She felt like a failure, and that was exactly when they saw their chance.

That was when the shadow seekers made their move, straight into the girls' minds.

*Looking for handouts,* a voice whispered mockingly inside Alex's throbbing head. *Welfare case. Loser. Do you think anyone wants you? Your own mother is glad that you rarely spend the night at home. You thought Elizabeth would save you from everything, give you a better life, but where's Elizabeth now, hmm? You get that she's never going to be herself again, right? You can't save her . . .*

"No!" Alex gasped. "That's not true."

But the other voice echoed strongly inside her, so much louder than her own pathetic little gasp. *Are you sure about that? Are you really sure?*

Beside Alex, with her arms wrapped tightly around Meteor's neck, Linda stood frozen as she frantically tried to conjure up the moon's magic. She remembered how she had done it the last time, how she had somehow managed to end up behind the moon and to hide there, in a place where no one could hurt her. She wanted to bring her friends with her now, away from the shadow seekers and their lies.

But . . . were they really lies? As Linda again failed to create a cool, round, full moon with her own thoughts, she collapsed in a heap, losing her glasses. That's when she heard the whispering. The whispering was coming from inside, from within herself.

*Stupid. The only thing you're any good at is reading, and now you can't even do that. You're going to fail, both at the moon magic and the Light Ceremony. And since your stupid friends are counting on the brainiac to give them all the right answers, people are going to die. You will, too, if you don't get out of here. There's still time. Time to give up like a real loser, because that's what you are. And you know it, don't you? Deep down inside? There's no point in resisting, Linda. That'll just make it harder for you later.*

Linda wavered. A group of shadow seekers saw their chance and went on the attack. She screamed loudly as she felt their sharp claws groping for her. Somewhere far away, Linda sensed a gleam of moonlight, the magic that wanted out, but it was blocked. The shadow seekers' bodies were dark gray, surrounded by a shroud of pink and hovering like a dense night fog. But there was nothing dark or hovering about the claws that suddenly tore into her jacket. Linda scrambled backward. It wasn't until she was already falling that she realized she was sliding down the embankment.

Right over the edge. Down into the abyss.

She screamed and clawed wildly with her fingernails, clinging to clumps of grass, dirt, and pebbles.

"Linda!" Lisa raced over and dove onto her stomach. Linda needed both hands to hold on, so Lisa didn't dare ask her to grab her hand. What if she couldn't pull her up . . . ? Instead she fumbled desperately for something, anything, that could help her get Linda back up. She managed to grab ahold of Linda's jacket. The fabric was damp and smooth under her shaking hands. She struggled and tugged while at the same time her friend fought to wriggle her way back up.

A shadow seeker stood behind them, so close that she could sense its nauseating, sickly-sweet scent, glaring at them with its glowing red eyes. Linda's eyes were wide with unmitigated panic.

*Rip.* A seam suddenly ripped in Linda's jacket. Lisa's heart was in her throat now. At least that's what it felt like.

"Come on!" Lisa yelled. "One, two, three. I'll pull and you crawl, slowly but surely. You're strong. You can do this!"

*But what about you?* the shadow seeker whispered into her ear. *You're doomed to lose everyone you love, one by one. What makes you think you can save Linda? You couldn't save your mother or your father. Your power is healing, and you're lucky that's the case, because you destroy everything that you touch, Lisa.*

The seams of Linda's jacket were barely holding. At the same time, it was like something clicked in Lisa's brain. It was now or never. She screamed at Linda, at the shadow seekers, and at the distorted voices that were trying to take over her. Her scream echoed down the stony embankment, right down over the cliff. "NO! I'm strong! I *can* help her! Come, Star, come!"

Starshine galloped over to the ledge. His beautiful head bent as he looked up at the sky. And then came the stars. They were in the sky and they were in Starshine's eyes. For one short, fleeting instant, Lisa was looking into them. And that instant was enough.

A gentle swirl of pink stardust spun in the air as Lisa grabbed around Linda's waist and managed to pull her up so that she had both arms up on top of the edge. Linda managed to wriggle the rest of the way up and then collapsed onto the ground. Lisa's whole body was shaking with adrenaline and relief. But she smiled when she saw her friend stand up, reach for her eyeglasses on the ground, and realize to her surprise that they weren't broken.

"I'd say thank you, but that seems so trivial," Linda mumbled and hugged her awkwardly.

Lisa shrugged slightly. There weren't any words that seemed right. She stroked Starshine's withers, feeling his heat radiating toward her.

*Thank you, my beloved horse. I don't know what you just did, but thank you.*

Reluctantly, she took her eyes off of her horse. Then she turned to Linda. "Come on. Time to send those shadow seekers back home to Pandoria."

The shadow seekers were growling drowsily from the water's edge. Anne stood beside them, her back straight, her feet apart.

"Do you see that?" Linda whispered to Lisa. "She doesn't even look scared."

Linda was pretty sure that Anne couldn't hear her. Even so, she thought she saw Anne's lips raise into a slight smile. That smile made Linda think of a beach. She had found Anne there, not that long ago, in a vision. And through the power of her mind, with the help of their strong bond of friendship, she was able to give Anne the support she needed to get out of Pandoria. Away from the shadow seekers and the awful whispering that seemed more and more true every time you heard it.

Now, by the cracking dam and the reservoir that was bursting at its banks, Anne said, "I'm not scared, because I know that that is exactly what they want. I know because I've encountered them before. You just need to ignore their lies. Then they can't hurt you. No matter what you do, don't let them sense that you're afraid. They feed on that. Fear is what sustains them. It gives them a way to get into your head."

Because that's where they wanted to go, the shadow seekers. Only once they were in there—in the most secret, inner space of all—could they cause their damage. Anne knew that, because they had managed to make it inside her head before, in Pandoria. And for a while she had believed the lies that they had whispered to her.

That she was worthless.

That she didn't have any real friends.

That the other Soul Riders wouldn't even try to help her.

That she and Concorde would die in Pandoria.

None of what they whispered had been true. And now Anne realized that there really weren't that many shadow seekers. Not now that she had taken a deep breath and forced herself to look right at the shadow seekers, really *look* at them.

It was the creatures' shadows, long and a variable pink hue, which made them look more numerous than they were. They danced along the wall, their reflections flickering in the purple-tinted water. They slipped away to get a running start and then crept forward with a low hissing noise. She watched how one of them approached Alex, who flapped her hands around wildly. Her eyes were tightly shut. It looked as if she was trying to shoo away a big insect.

No one made bug repellent strong enough for this kind of pest though, Anne thought. There was only one thing that could help.

"Good, Alex," she yelled. "Shut them out. Just drive them away! They can't hurt you if you don't let them in your head. You need to get them out of there, do you hear me? *Out!*"

The air was still. A faint, buzzing sound had chased away the water noise. Anne stared at the shadow seekers without moving.

The biggest one—*the leader,* Anne thought—approached her quickly and purposefully. It stopped right in front of her and reached out a blurry hand toward her face.

Anne could almost swear she saw the hideous thing smile. Its red eyes glowed. Anger welled up inside of her, making her dare to act.

"I don't plan to let you threaten me again, do you get that?!" Anne howled right into the shadow seeker's face. "Get lost, scram!"

The shadow seeker lunged forward, grabbing her legs with its hideous, coiling hands. Anne felt like she was falling into the water. The roar of the water was coming uncomfortably close now. She saw Concorde kicking at some of the prying shadow seekers, and she had an idea.

"Concorde!" she yelled. Her big, gray horse pricked up his ears, aimed yet another kick at the creatures and then galloped over to her. When he was standing close enough that she could touch him, she started to conjure the Sun Circle. It was slower than the last time. Resisting the shadow seekers stole so much of her energy. But now, with Concorde so close to her, it was easier.

Suddenly the icy chill of the water was gone. She felt the sun growing inside her, warming her and making her powerful.

She shook the shadow creature off of herself and stood up. Concorde lay down on the ground so that she could mount him more easily. Once she was settled on his back, she knew it was time.

The Sun Circle was strong, strong enough to push away the shadow seekers. She stared at them again and saw how the creatures backed away. In the reflection in their eyes, she saw her own eyes glowing like two big suns. The sun vibrated, made of gasses, shooting sharp rays out of her eyes. The hissing creatures slowly dwindled. They lost their contours, their color, and their form just as before in Pandoria.

Soon, only their leader was left. The leader didn't seem to be affected by the sun's magic at all. The creature sniffed and hissed, looking at Anne and Concorde with something that almost resembled curiosity.

Over by the ledge, they heard a bellow as Alex tried to hit the shadow seeker with her lightning. She was growing more confident now, and she felt stronger as she summoned the power of the Lightning Circle. Anne turned around and watched a confetti rain of lightning, stars, and crescent moons shoot through the air. She smiled broadly. Then she yelled, "Come here! All together now, at the same time!"

The shadow seeker snarled and made a hissing lunge at Anne and Concorde, but Lisa's stardust thwarted it. A bolt of lightning darted by and stabbed the creature in the leg. Its scream pierced through the air and rang through their ears, but they continued.

The sun was everywhere now. Yellow and white, powerful and flaming, it pushed the shadow seeker away, closer to the dam. The air trembled once again. Time stood still.

There was a crunching sound coming from one of the cracks in the dam. Suddenly a brilliant pink light flowed out of the crack.

Then, the last shadow seeker crawled into the crack, into the pink light.

Before it disappeared, it gave one last, weak shriek. The shriek turned into an echo that turned into a whisper.

Then it was gone.

The Soul Riders were left standing there with their horses, watching the sun's rays fade away. Soon, the world was gray again, aside from the pink cracks in the dam. They looked at each other and laughed in disbelief.

"What *was* that?" Alex said, rubbing her hair.

"Sun magic, ladies," Anne replied with a smile. "Concorde helped me there at the end. I've never felt it so strongly before. I think the sun was even shining out of my eyes for a bit. Crazy."

"Yeah, that's really taking the expression *if looks could kill* to a whole other level," Lisa said. They all giggled. Anne rested her head against Concorde and inhaled his horsey scent. She felt the feeling of unreality slowly ebbing away. Her eyes were a little tender and sore, but no worse than they usually felt after she'd sat at her computer studying for a long time.

All this new, magical stuff that she was trying get a handle on. She was so happy that she had the others to talk to. And Concorde, of course, her beloved Concorde. Had he just saved them?

For a while, they all stood there together, with their heads resting on their horses. It took some effort to move on. It was so tempting to just remain here in the moment, but finally it was time.

"You know what we have to do now, right?" Linda said, running her hand over the white blaze on Meteor's muzzle. "It's time for the Light Ceremony. That's why we came here, after all. The shadow seekers were just an unnecessary step along the way."

"Oh, please, can't we wait just a little bit longer?" Lisa asked, stroking Starshine's muzzle. "I'm still pretty shaky. I don't know if I'm up to it."

"Uh," Alex said. "I don't really think we have a choice. You see that?"

And then they saw the water level rising even more, horrifically fast, splashing their feet, soaking their riding pants, which felt cold and sticky against their skin. The horses were dragging their hooves and whinnying loudly. Tin-Can showed the whites of his eyes and shook his head with quick, jerking movements.

*Krikelin doesn't like the water*, Lisa thought and shivered.

"Alex is right," Anne said. "We can't wait any longer. The shadow seekers seem to have made the cracks between here and Pandoria even bigger."

Linda picked up the Light Ceremony book, letting the golden gleam shine on their tired faces for a brief second. Then she nodded slowly. "Yes," she said, her voice somber. "It's time now."

**8**

They all felt it, how the thin mountain air thickened, sweeping in and surrounding them. Everything felt heavy and charged. The already dark clouds looked almost black now. Thunder rumbled over the mountains, and deep down, inside the water beneath the dam, they heard a gurgling sound, as if someone had pulled the stopper up from the bathtub drain. The girls looked at each other, wide-eyed, as Linda opened the Light Ceremony book and began to read.

She read about the light that the girl on horseback—the first of many—shone upon the island so that everything that was once cold and dead was restored to life.

She read about the light that was meant to balance out the darkness. About the Soul Riders, whose job it was to make sure the balance was maintained. It was so hard to fathom that she was reading about the four of them.

She read spells and incantations written in old-fashioned words she didn't know. The others stood near the water's edge, in a circle. The cracks ran along the sides of the dam, and they were so big now that they were visible to the naked eye. In some places, it just looked like cracked cement. In others, a dazzling pink glow shone through.

"Why are they pink?" Lisa wondered. "They were pink before, too, when the shadow seekers vanished down into them."

"Pandorian cracks," Anne explained. "It's the Pandorian energy leaking into our world. There are cracks like these, too, on the other side in Pandoria, but they're green."

"Because our world is leaking into theirs?" Linda guessed.

"Exactly," Anne nodded. Her cheeks felt warm from the feeling of finally being listened to and taken seriously. It was strange, she thought, but in a way her friends' confidence warmed her more than the sunshine that had just recently been beaming from her own eyes.

*Humans before magic. So it must be. Everything else is wrong. But now: magic. Again.*

They all held hands and kept close to their horses, so close that they could feel the heat from their bodies. The horses' heat spread among them as they squeezed each other's hands. Lisa felt how Starshine leaned his head toward her shoulder. As he did that, she saw a cloud of small, swirling stars in all the colors of the rainbow slowly rise into the sky. The swirl of stars seemed to come from inside Starshine's big, shining eyes, or maybe from the heat that radiated between them. It wasn't electricity, but something softer. She didn't know how, but she understood that the horses were also meant to be part of the ceremony.

"Do you feel that?" she whispered to Alex, who was standing closest to her. "The horses . . . they're participating. They're helping us."

Alex looked at Tin-Can and lovingly admired his long, unruly forelock that almost covered his dark eyes, which always had a mischievous glint in them. His surprisingly noble head was always held upright, proud and a little cocky. She let go of Lisa's hand and put it on Tin-Can's withers. When her hand touched Tin-Can, it sparked. Her horse whinnied softly as a series of small, squiggly bolts of lightning flew up into the sky. She smiled in gratitude toward her horse before she grasped Lisa's hand and squeezed it gently. "Yes," she said. "Of course I feel it. They're guiding us now." Alex glanced up at the sky where the edges of the clouds were just barely lined with stars and lightning. Soon, she saw only the clouds again, but she felt it. Something was about to happen. The magic—their magic—had been set in motion. Nothing could stop it now.

*It's working*, Linda thought, feeling warmth from deep within. Then she went back to reading. Everything was adrenaline. Everything was *now*. There was no later, not yet.

Sometimes she would get tripped up and need to start over. But after a while, she found her rhythm. Her voice blended with the others. A ray of sunshine broke through the heavy cloud cover. Before anyone could say anything, Anne lifted up her hand and caught the sunbeam, which danced softly in the palm of her hand. The ray of light grew with her touch, one beam at a time. It was as if Anne were weaving light out of the sun's rays. In the end, the light was so big that it reached all the way to Lisa's hand, which was clinging tightly to Anne's.

Linda read on. She took a deep breath as she saw how the light Anne was creating was now filled with stars. They twinkled inside the scorching, hazy brightness.

"Wow, that really got hot!" Lisa said, wiping her forehead.

Lisa was right. It was suddenly so hot that they had to take off their jackets. The fall chill was gone. The air exuded a sweaty, midsummer heat. The heat rose, making the water in the dam bubble.

Alex felt the heat from her pendant and grimaced.

"Linda?" she said. "Are you sure we're doing this right? Is it really supposed to be this hot?"

"I don't know," Linda replied without looking up from the book.

"It feels stable," Anne said. But she couldn't help but smile when she saw how the sunlight reached Alex, and within it, the stars formed a zigzag-like lightning pattern.

Alex captured the sparking ball of light. Then, she passed it on, looking amazed at how it grew in the air as it passed Concorde, lightly grazing his short, shimmering gray mane. It was as if the mere presence of the horses helped support the magic, sustained it, and then intensified it.

Meteor pricked up his ears and passed the magical, crackling flow of energy along with a nod of his muzzle. Meteor's gentle, friendly eyes sparkled at Alex as their eyes met.

*It's us*, she thought. *We're doing this, together.*

Tin-Can snorted quietly behind her.

They helped Linda hold the book so that she had one hand free, and then they all read together. A silvery moon now formed inside the web of light. It was as if the moon's presence cooled it down. Linda could almost swear that she heard a faint fizzling sound as the moon met the sun.

Hot and cold.

Sun and moon.

So totally different, and yet in harmony. Just like her and Anne.

Around them, the blue and pink energy crackled. The light pulsated in time with their voices. Lisa started singing, an evocative, timeless lullaby. It felt strangely familiar somehow. The others started singing, realizing that they knew the words. Linda set the book down, and with their hands raised to the sky, they launched the light that they had created into the heavens. The heat vibrated between them as they sang. As long as the light grew and moved with them, surely they were doing something right?

They fumbled their way along, together. Anne's voice cracked several times as she tried to keep up with how high Lisa was singing. She laughed self-consciously. Lisa just shook her head and squeezed her hand, got her to keep singing even though her voice was cracking. Anne's eyes filled with tears as a memory emerged from the recesses of her mind. The sun's rays made her tears sparkle as they surfaced in her eyes.

They were singing in an ancient language that none of them recognized. Their clear song rose into the sky, mixing with the gleaming light that was dancing around them at an ever-increasing tempo. Then, gradually—none of them knew how much time had passed—the pale pink light changed color. It became a blinding white glare, as strong as fluorescent lighting. The net of light arced across the sky, over the dam, over the girls and their horses.

Everything was hot, crackling energy.

The song was over. It was oppressively quiet.

The rays of light left the sky colorless, translucent.

The pink was gone. The world was gray again.

*Either this is the end of the world*, Alex thought, *or we succeeded.*

They were still standing in a circle, and they let it remain unbroken a little while longer. The air felt cool and comfortable to breathe. The sun shining above them was a completely normal sun. No stars, no lightning, no moon.

"We did it," Alex whispered. "We actually did it."

"Mhmm," Linda said. "But I have no idea how."

"Does it matter?" Anne said. "I mean, it worked."

"It was as if something took us over, wasn't it?" Lisa said, resting her sweaty forehead against Starshine's neck. "Like we suddenly knew how, even though we didn't have any idea how to do it."

"The magic was from the Light Ceremony book," Linda said.

"Yes, of course," Alex replied. "But not just that. To be totally honest, I think it was us. Well, us and the horses together. They knew what we needed to do before we understood it."

"It's always been us," Anne said, gazing wide-eyed at Concorde.

Tin-Can snorted his agreement. Alex let go of her friends' hands and patted her horse with her sticky, trembling hands.

"You all heard the man," she quipped. "The boss agrees."

"What do you think the boss will say to riding on out of here and setting up camp somewhere in the forest?" Anne asked with a big yawn. "I don't know about you guys, but I'm starving. And exhausted!"

The others murmured their agreement. Except for Linda.

"Wait," she said. "How do we know that it's safe to leave this spot and just . . . ride away? Are the cracks . . ." She leaned forward and critically scrutinized the wall of the dam, observing that it was still cracked. "What if it breaks even though the magic is gone?"

"It'll be fine," replied Anne, who had once again assumed the role of leader in a sort of spur-of-the-moment, offhand way. "This dam seems like it's been here for eons and as long as the cracks aren't getting any worse, I'm sure it will probably continue to stand here for a long time to come. Besides, I bet the dam has an engineer or someone who can deal with the cracks that are left . . ."

"Yeah, yeah, it's *safe*," Lisa said emphatically. "Come on, we're going now!"

Alex thought she heard something sharp and impatient in Lisa's voice that she didn't recognize. She furrowed her brow and gave her friend a questioning look.

"Why are you suddenly in such a hurry?" Alex wondered. "We don't need to ride right back to the Stone Circle right away, do we? I mean, hello, we just finished the Light Ceremony! The dam didn't burst! Why can't we just, I don't know, like, chill a little?"

Lisa shook her head impatiently and started fiddling with the stirrup leathers on Starshine's saddle. Her hand shook a little against the leather, but her voice was steady as she said, "I need to ask you for a huge favor, far too big of a favor, actually. I know that, and I also know that the timing really sucks after what we just did. But I have to ask anyway. And I have to ask you to listen."

"Lisa . . . ?" Linda said, looking puzzled.

Lisa gulped. She looked back and forth between the three girls, her lower lip trembling. Then her whole face sunk, and she sobbed, "I have to rescue my father! He's trapped inside Dark Core Headquarters, being held captive by Mr. Sands. He must have seen or heard something that he shouldn't have, and now he's in the clutches of that horrible villain. We have to save him! And I need your help. Please? We can't wait any longer."

# 9

Everyone's eyes turned to Lisa.

"I understand that you want to help your father," Anne began cautiously. "Believe me, I totally get that. But . . . are you sure it's a good idea to rush into it now? We don't know what we're facing."

Lisa wiped her eyes, only to feel how fast her tears were falling now.

"I need to do this," Lisa said between sobs. "And I need do it now. Don't you think I've waited long enough?" she added. "What if Mr. Sands were holding one of your parents prisoner?! Don't tell me that you would wait, because I don't believe you! You would have rushed off to help before now, I know you would."

The star-shaped birthmark on her cheek sparkled faintly from her tears. Anne patted her gently on the shoulder and could feel how much Lisa was shaking.

"Lisa," Alex sighed, "I understand that you're worried about your dad. Of course you are. You know that we would like nothing more than to be able to help you. One for all and all for one, you know? But, forgive me for saying this, riding over there without a plan is a terrible idea. Don't you understand that that's exactly what Mr. Sands wants, for us to ride straight into his trap? How are we going to deal with all the guards when we get there? Seriously, my head hurts just thinking about this right now. It just won't work,

Lisa, not right now, anyway! Can't you see that? We need to think this through."

When Lisa listened to Alex it was like something caught fire inside her. Even before the words were out in the air, she regretted them. But by then it was already too late.

"I'm *so sorry* that my petty family worries are such an inconvenience to you," Lisa snapped. "I forgot that you don't care about anyone other than yourself, well, and Tin-Can of course. It's not like family is something that even matters to you. Your mom and siblings don't even know where you are right now, do they? You just run away from anything tough without any concern for what, or who, you're leaving behind. But you know I'm not like you, Alex. And I'm happy about that."

Her words cut into Alex like red-hot knives. Listening to Lisa hurt so much it practically took Alex's breath away. Then she let the anger take over.

"No, just no . . . !" Alex snarled, letting go of Tin-Can's reins and lunging at Lisa.

"Alex!" Linda said in warning. "It's not worth it." She intercepted Alex and caught her, restraining her forcibly in her arms.

"Let go of me!" Alex yelled. But Linda didn't let go of Alex. Instead she held on tightly until Alex gave up struggling. Alex was strong, but so was Linda—much stronger than she looked. Her body was soft and curvy, but all those hours on horseback had given her muscles in places she hadn't even realized you could have muscles. The lactic acid was coursing through her tensed arm muscles as Alex tried to wriggle out of Linda's anaconda-like hold. They were so close that Linda could smell the pungent scent of sweat, dirt, and horse. Something was burning against her jacket that made her wince. It was Alex's necklace, smoldering against her upper arm.

"All right," Linda said, running her hand over Alex's hair. "Breathe. We can't afford to fight right now. Please, Alex, calm down. For my sake. And for yours."

The mean words and the screaming slowly abated. Finally, the only sound was faint, forlorn sobbing. Lisa was crying, too. Her tears left her face red and blotchy.

"I'm sorry, Alex," Lisa whimpered. "That's not what I meant. I never meant to . . ."

Anne stood there in complete silence, just staring with her mouth open. *What's going on?* she thought. *What on Earth is going on? A minute ago, we were standing here creating magic together. How did everything fall apart so quickly?* She leaned her face against Concorde's neck, pretending to tighten the throat latch on his bridle. Her heart was racing. She inhaled the scent of decaying leaves and slightly sweaty horse, waiting for someone to say something, something that would make everything all right again and take away the hurtful words, something nice. But no one said anything. The silence felt suffocating. Seconds passed, and then minutes.

"Don't talk to me right now," Alex finally said, her voice muffled against Linda's jacket. "Just keep quiet, Lisa."

Without looking at Lisa, Alex freed herself from Linda's arms. She pulled her hands over her cheeks, took a few gulps of water from the bottle in her saddlebag. Then she mounted Tin-Can. Her lips were pursed into a narrow line.

"Alex is right. I don't think there's any point in talking any more right now," Linda said. "We're all tired and hungry. We need to rest. Come on. Let's head out of here before it gets totally dark and pitch camp as quickly as we can."

Lisa wiped away her tears with her shirt sleeve and nodded slowly. She didn't look in Alex's direction as she mounted Starshine, but she made sure to ride behind Tin-Can so that they could talk when Alex was ready.

Linda and Anne mounted their horses as well, and then they were off.

It was starting to get dark. In the little village down below, a warm yellow glow shone from the windows and streetlamps. People were starting their evenings: clearing their tables after dinner, doing their dishes, telling their children to do a good job brushing their teeth. Everyday life was continuing, as if nothing had happened. Even though tragedy had been so narrowly avoided. *I wonder how many times we get so close to disaster without knowing it,* Linda wondered, running her hand over Meteor's coarse mane. It glistened in the twilight, lit by the lights from the houses down below. *Maybe it happens all the time, every day. We just don't know about it. Is it true what people say, that what you don't know can't hurt you?*

A prolonged howl came from the dense, dark forest. Was that a wolf? Or . . . something else?

"I wonder where the Dark Riders are now," Linda mumbled.

"I wonder that, too," said Anne, pulling her jacket more tightly around her.

"I think they're out there somewhere," Linda said, asking Meteor to trot with a squeeze of her legs. "All three of them: Sabine, Jessica, and Katja. What if they're just waiting to strike?"

"Or they're still lying at the bottom of the ravine, unable to hurt us anymore," Alex said, her voice harsh. "I know which one I'm voting for. Come, let's gallop a little!"

They broke into a gallop, one by one. When they slowed down again, Lisa trotted up to Alex so that they were riding side by side. She picked a pine needle out of Starshine's blue mane. She sighed a little, silently, she hoped. Then she tentatively said, "Ceasefire?"

Silence. Alex broke into a gallop and pulled away. Lisa galloped after her, yelling into the wind so that it echoed. She could hear how shrill her own voice sounded and she made a face.

"Alex, I feel terrible about saying that stuff. I shouldn't have said it, but I can't think about anything except for my dad being there at Dark Core Headquarters. I know you have a dad, too, even though you haven't seen him for a long time. I know you understand how scared and lonely I feel right now."

Alex was still quiet, but she had slowed to a trot.

Lisa continued, "He needs our help now, just like Starshine needed my help before. I saved Starshine, and I'm going to save my dad, too. But I need your help to do it. Although . . . I need for you to forgive me first, Alex! I don't want to be enemies. Please, I need you!"

Silence again. The seconds ticked by and turned into minutes. Finally, Alex quietly said, "Linda was right about what she said before. We can't afford to fight right now. Of course I forgive you, Lisa. We both said stupid stuff."

Lisa exhaled. She felt her tense shoulders sinking back into place. "So, you're coming?"

"I didn't say *that*," Alex said. "We'll have to talk about that later. But that ceasefire you mentioned? Yes to that. Fighting is so exhausting, especially with your best friends."

"Good," Lisa replied. "And, hey? Thank you."

*Best friends.* The words touched her. No one had ever called Lisa their best friend before. She rode on with her eyes shining and a warm, cozy feeling in her chest.

At the first house down in the village below, a little boy listened to his evening lullaby with his toy horse clutched tightly in his hand.

Life goes on.

· ✦ · ✦ · ✦ ·

A few hours later, they were sitting at their campsite and eating a late dinner. The night was cold, but the heat from the campfire they had just managed to keep lit helped—a little, anyway. Above them the sky was velvety black, and the stars were out shining brightly. The horses stood grazing under the tall pines. A snoring sound revealed that at least one of them had already fallen asleep. Probably Tin-Can, Alex thought. He snored the loudest of all the horses at Jorvik Stables.

Anne tossed a branch onto the fire. As the flames flared up, she thought of the sun that had shone from her eyes as she had fought the shadow seekers. The memory made her shiver. It was still so strange to think about. Instead she kept feeding the fire, happy to have a simple job to do for once.

"I just thought of something," she said. "All the stuff we're doing now, the whole Soul Rider thing. We're doing it all in secret. The people in that village down there are never going to find out what we did, what could have happened. And that father we talked to, he probably told everyone down there about the crazy teenagers who came riding up, yelling that the dam was going to break. Since it never did, he was right about that in a way. The way other people will see it."

"You can't think about it like that," Linda said. "Does a tree fall in the forest if no one hears it fall? Of course it does! What we're doing has to take place in silence. That's the whole point."

"Yeah, I know," Anne said. "I'm just so used to thinking about what other people think all the time."

She looked into the fire and thought about her family, who were surely asleep back home—her mother, father, and little brother. They had no idea what she was up to right now. But still . . .

Sometimes Anne felt like she wanted to tell her mother absolutely everything. She actually thought that she would understand. Yes, she was quite certain that her mother knew more than she let on. There was something about the look in her eyes. Several times when her mother thought Anne was sleeping, she would come and sit on the edge of her bed and sort of . . . watch over her. As if she instinctively understood that Anne needed someone to keep watch. It happened most often at night, when she wished she could talk to her mother, really talk about everything that was secret and difficult. Then in the morning her mother would be her usual, slightly cool self. The distance was somehow there between them again, and Anne didn't know if she had it in her to try to get close to her mother again. It was so hard.

With a sigh, Anne looked away from the fire to her friends. In the glow of the campfire, Lisa's eyes looked almost feverish. She looked almost sick, Anne thought.

"Is everything okay, Lisa?" Anne wondered, putting a hand on Lisa's arm.

"Yeah," Lisa responded, flinching at the unexpected touch, but then she nodded quickly, a little too quickly, perhaps. Then she looked around the campfire, looking at her friends one by one. "And what about us?" she continued. "Are we okay? I mean, for real? I said a bunch of really stupid things to Alex, but she says that she's forgiven me. She's actually the only one who's said anything about me wanting us to ride to Dark Core to help my dad. Did the rest of you even hear what I said? Because I'm starting to wonder."

When her friends took too long to answer, Lisa looked around the campfire at them again, one by one. She tried to read their faces, lit up by the flames.

Anne was fiddling with a lock of hair that had fallen out of her high, tight ponytail. She was winding her blond hair around her

61

finger, loop after loop, all the way up to her knuckles, so tight that they turned white. Her face was half-turned away from the light, closed off. *Why is she so hard to read?* Lisa wondered. *What do I need to do to get through to her?*

Linda chewed on her lower lip and stared into the fire. Her lips moved slowly, as if she was rehearsing something that she wasn't quite brave enough to say out loud yet. *She's working up the courage to say no.* The realization hit Lisa like a hard fist. She felt her stomach contract.

Only Alex looked her in the eye. For a while they just looked at each other. Lisa noticed that Alex had a dark rim around her light brown eyes, and streaks of gold and green in her iris. There was something almost cat-like about her eyes, Lisa thought. They were so changeable and alive.

They shared so much now. Together they were carrying the whole world, the balance between good and evil. They had just prevented a disaster from taking place. Even though they didn't actually know each other all that well, she thought. Apparently, she hardly even knew what color their eyes were.

"I still don't think it's a good idea," Alex said, squirming. "It's too dangerous, and it feels a little too much like a trap. But *if* it's a trap, I assume it would be better if we all ride there together. Then maybe we would still stand a chance. And I understand why we have to do it. I haven't seen my father in a really long time, but if I knew that he was in danger . . ." She swallowed, looking into the flames. "I would think about it the same way you are. I know that."

Lisa exhaled. The knot in her stomach slowly relaxed.

"Thank you," Lisa said. Then she turned to the others. "Anne?" she asked cautiously. "Linda?"

Silence. The sound of a hooting owl filled the night. Anne released the coils of hair and started over again. Behind her round eyeglasses, Linda's eyes were almost as black as the sky and just as mysterious.

"Okay, then," Linda said. "Okay. But we have to be careful. And another thing, an important thing. There is no way that we are separating again. We saw how that went before. We have to help each other. So, yes, we're going. Right?"

Linda looked expectantly at Anne. She had stopped fiddling with her hair now. A tense, heavy silence settled between them. Everyone was waiting for Anne to say something.

"You know what?" Anne finally said. "It really sucks to be the one who hesitates, the coward. I hate that this is how it is."

She remembered a day at the beach when she was little: big waves, blue sky, and the hot, broiling sun; grains of itchy sand sticking everywhere; the feeling of wanting to plunge into the waves and become one with the sea. But her mother said no. It was too dangerous to swim right after eating—you could get cramps! Anne knew now that that wasn't true, but she remembered so clearly how it felt. She sat next to her mother on the towel, hot and grumpy and covered in little grains of sand while the other kids played happily in the water.

The others were watching her attentively.

She kept talking, feeling her cheeks redden.

"It really sucks to always play that role, always be the one who says no. I'm sure you think that I don't care as much as you guys, but that's not true! I care. I just need a little more time."

"Anne," Alex said softly. "You're the bravest person I know."

Anne's surprised laugh echoed across the campsite.

"Uh, what?" Anne gasped. "You can't be serious."

"Yeah," Alex said with a nod. "If it weren't for you, we wouldn't have driven away the shadow seekers. And if we hadn't done that, then we never would have been able to keep the dam from breaking."

"Alex is right," Lisa said. "Sometimes there are these things you have to hear about yourself over and over again. You know, the kinds of things that people say about you? Like the stories people tell, only people take them seriously. *Lisa is so fragile. You have to be careful with her. She's had such a hard time, poor thing.*"

The fire crackled as Lisa tossed a pebble into it. She took a shaky breath before continuing.

"You hear it so often that in the end you start to believe it. Finally, you end up seeing yourself as fragile and weak. You notice the cracks forming time after time. Even though you're actually strong, because that's how you deal with hardships, by cracking again and again. But you start believing the story about yourself. And then you turn into that fragile little Lisa that everyone talks about so cautiously. Little porcelain doll Lisa whose mother died. *Handle with care.* It turns into . . . what do you call that again, Linda? A self-fulfilling prophecy?"

"Exactly," Linda nodded. "Lisa's right. I'm terrified, too, Anne. Believe me. I want nothing more than to gallop back home and hide in my bed with my cat and a really big book, to just forget all of this and let someone else take care of it. But we can't do that. Deep down inside you know that, too."

"I know," Anne responds. "And I understand exactly what you mean, Lisa. I'm coming with you. I mean, of course I am. It's us against the world, right?"

"Us against the world," the others said in unison.

"Plus, you're not like a porcelain doll at all," Alex told Lisa. "You remind me more of those old rag dolls my mother played with when she was little. With messy red hair and all. Raggedy Lisa."

"Oh, shut up!" Lisa blurted out and slugged Alex's arm. But she was laughing as she did it.

"Shh!" Linda suddenly hissed, looking around. "Did you guys hear that?"

"What?" Anne said sleepily.

"In the woods. It sounded like a horse."

"I didn't hear anything," Lisa said.

"Me either," Alex said. "I'm sure it was just Meteor having a nightmare about us running out of oats."

Linda stood up, walked past the sleeping horses, and listened for sounds in the trees. Nothing. She exhaled and sat down on her sleeping bag close to Anne, who had already crawled into her own sleeping bag.

"You're probably right," she said. "I'm sure it was nothing. But I'm going to stay awake and stand guard for a while just to be on the safe side."

*Staying awake after this long day is harder than I thought it was going to be,* Linda sighed to herself as she stood watch. It wasn't even that late yet, but after the day they had, she was feeling completely drained. It didn't help that the other three girls were sleeping that kind of deep, almost unconscious sleep that only the truly exhausted can sleep. In an effort to stay awake, she stood up and jumped up and down, doing as many jumping jacks as she could manage. Then, when she felt like she was going to die from the boredom and the cold, she took a flashlight and went to take a look around behind the nearest line of trees. The silence was every bit as dense and compact as the darkness in the forest. Even so, she couldn't shake the sense that someone was watching them.

Goosebumps never lied. Neither did her intuition. But finally, the hair on her arms relaxed. She started breathing normally. Everything was still quiet.

Fifteen minutes passed, and then another fifteen minutes. Linda stifled yet another yawn and got comfortable in her sleeping bag. She listened for sounds, but all she could hear was the other girls' faint snores.

"Eh," she said to herself. "They were probably right. It was nothing."

She sank deeper into the sleeping bag and immediately fell asleep.

Deeper in the forest, a branch broke under the weight of a horse's hooves. Since the Soul Riders were asleep, none of them heard the sound. None of them heard the big, black horse give a rumbling neigh, either, low and powerful, like thunder in a rain-laden sky. And no one heard his rider—a tall girl with a coal-black braid slung over one shoulder and a scar across her face—as she hissed, "Shh, Khaan! Don't ruin the surprise. Not yet . . ."

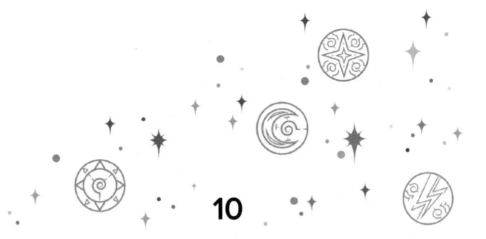

# 10

Through the thick black of the night, three riders slowly made their way through the forest. Apart from the muted glow that came from their horses' hooves, everything around them was shrouded in darkness. All of Jorvik was asleep. But in one of the trees, a large spider spun her web. Quickly and methodically she moved back and forth. The fragile threads gleamed in the moonlight.

Beyond the trail, the glow of a campfire could be seen in the distance. The riders turned to look at it. For a brief moment, they seemed to hesitate. Their horses slowed. Then, one of the riders shook her head. "We'll wait," she said, shortening her reins. The other two nodded, almost imperceptibly, and they all sped up into a gallop. Farther in among the trees, a wolf sank its sharp teeth into its prey. A brief cry of surprise, that was all–a stifled whimper. Then everything was quiet again. At the nearby campsite, where four girls and their horses were sound asleep, the campfire dwindled.

Midnight came and went. Soon the hour before dawn, "the hour of the wolf," as it was known, arrived. It was said that it was the hour when the most people died. An hour when feelings of loneliness become so heavy that you falter under the burden, that brief period just before everyone wakes up from their sleep.

Everything was silent and dark; everything was dormant, slumbering, waiting.

It was the ideal hour for the hunter. While the prey sleeps, the wild animal approaches.

The three riders settled into a fierce canter. Sabine rode in the lead. Her face felt tight and she scratched her cheek in irritation. It was bruised and covered with thick scabs. It itched like crazy.

When she and Khaan had fallen from the stone bridge, they had fallen headfirst. A human body could never have survived that fall, but Sabine had never been human. Thank goodness.

She wished more than ever that she could be like the snake that slithered along the path. She wanted to shed her skin and move on, get rid of this tight, disgusting human costume, and become her own true self again.

Soon, she told herself. As soon as they managed to lure the Soul Riders and their horses to them so that they could steal their magical energy. Then they could finally liberate Garnok and release him once and for all.

"Everything for Garnok, right?" she mumbled into the night.

No one responded.

"I said, everything for Garnok," Sabine hissed.

"Everything for Garnok," the others finally echoed.

"And down with the Soul Riders," Jessica added, rubbing her temple. An enormous black eye extended well up onto her forehead. "They will have to pay for what they did. Did they really think they could outride us like that? They think they've won, but victory will be ours."

"Exactly," Sabine muttered and cast a quick glance over her shoulder. Jessica rode behind her and then, bringing up the rear, just as gleaming white as the night is black, rode Katja. Her face was ghostly pale in the nighttime darkness. The very night felt colder when you were near Katja, because she sent a chill over everything that got in her way. If Sabine was a glowing ember, Katja was an ice axe. Just as icy cold and deadly. Jessica rode in the middle, which Sabine found significant. Even though they had known each other forever, in a way that transcended even time and space, Sabine still had a hard time coming to grips with Jessica. She was cooler than Sabine—which certainly wasn't hard to accomplish—but also slipperier, more evasive somehow. She had an easier time blending in with people. She seemed to have picked up some of that hopeless longing to fit in that most humans had. Maybe those were the traits that made her the perfect general. It was hard for Sabine to wrap her mind around. She scratched like crazy at her cheek again and screamed when her fingernails tore into her skin, drawing blood.

"What the . . . ?" she mumbled, looking at her own hands. Since, like all predators, she had perfect night vision, she had no problem seeing in the dark. By this point she was almost used to seeing her hands look tame and human-like. So, she gasped when she noticed the claws.

Claws, not hands. Her true form. When the shock wore off, she laughed, a deep, relieved laugh that made Jessica look at her with an angry furrow in her brow. Sabine kept looking at her claws, which had a convulsive grasp on the reins. They were twisted, black, and razor sharp, just as she remembered them. The blood glistened as she wiggled her claws. Something which—if she recognized the emotion—could be described as happiness welled up in her chest.

She had missed them. She had missed being herself.

But as the moon sailed into view through the treetops, her claws were gone again. Her hands were once more adorned by ordinary, pathetic human fingernails. Black and sharp, sure, but still fingernails. She shook her head sadly and urged her horse onward. Khaan shook his heavy head and champed at the bit. Their dark ride continued.

The silence between the three riders was so thick that you could have cut it with a knife. Sabine tightened her reins and urged Khaan along. She thought of Mr. Sands, waiting at the portal. And then she smiled, a tense, nasty smile that made her taut skin feel like it might crack. She made a face. Her throat felt tight and narrow when she swallowed.

"What do you think?" Sabine asked. "Should we ride back and surprise them in their camp? Scare them a little?"

"That would be fun," Katja replied mischievously. Her white eyes glowed in the dark. For an instant, it was possible to make out the contours of a skull behind her expressionless face. "But it would probably be best to wait. They'll come to headquarters on their own soon enough. I've heard Lisa crying for her father at night. She's planning on trying to rescue him. Soon."

"Poor little girl," Jessica said with a laugh. "Straight into the trap. Again. They have the memory of a goldfish, those four."

"Lucky for us," Katja purred.

Something inside Sabine started itching, just as intensely as the itch on her cheek. "Do you really think they're crazy enough to ride straight into the heart of darkness? You think they're going to try to break the girl's father out? I'm not so sure . . ."

Jessica and Katja were right. It would be ideal if the Soul Riders went to Dark Core's headquarters under their own power, and soon. There were so many things that needed to be set into motion. They had no time to waste! But at the same time, she hated the thought of agreeing with the other two. She wasn't planning to let anyone lead her.

"No," Sabine said. "I don't think that's where they're going. Not yet. But," she added, feeling how her smile made her face feel tight again, "it would certainly be fun if they tried."

Jessica stretched her long, slender neck. Something flashed in her eyes. "Yes, think, just think, if all four of them came. With their horses. That would be almost too good to be true, almost . . ."

Sabine turned back around and looked at Jessica. Now, when her face was lit by the moonlight, Sabine saw that Jessica's eyes weren't blue at all, the way they had been a moment ago. They were yellow, like the eyes of a hungry wolf—and her pupils, which had just a moment ago been dilated and shiny black, were now narrow slits, like those of a snake. Maybe they weren't as different as she thought, she and Jessica, all things considered . . .

Jessica's throaty laugh echoed against the rustling of the trees. The Dark Riders rode on, further into the hour of the wolf.

**11**

None of them were really sure who had woken up first. All they knew was that suddenly they were awake, all four of them. The night air was bitingly cold despite their thick sleeping bags. Their breath was visible as cloudy puffs of white in the darkness.

"What was that?" Lisa asked, sitting up. "Did you guys hear that?"

Alex sat up as well and pulled her knit cap lower over her forehead. Then she peered out into the darkness, listening carefully.

"It sounded like a branch breaking," Alex said. "Like footsteps. Someone *is* here, out in the forest."

The goosebumps on Linda's arm were back now.

They heard the cracking sound again, the sound of footsteps approaching. And then something flickering and shining, a light of some sort.

A bright, golden-white light fell on their faces. In the shadows, the contours of a large human body towered before them. The body took a step forward, straight toward their campsite and their fading fire.

That's when they started screaming.

# 12

The figure emerged from the darkness. At first only a long shadow was visible. Then, the shadow took on a face, a voice. It said, "Pardon me, girls. I didn't mean to scare you. It's just me, Avalon."

He raised his lantern to his face to show them. Linda clasped her hands to her face and moaned out loud.

"Avalon!" Linda exclaimed. "Oh my God, you scared us to death! What are you doing here?"

The druid smiled tentatively and set down his lantern. Then, he sat down by their campfire and poked at the dying embers to rouse the flames back to life.

"I was looking for you four, actually," Avalon said. "I tried to catch up to you, but when I got to the dam, you weren't there. How did the ceremony go? I saw that you managed to use the magic at the dam, but how did it feel, you know? That's some pretty powerful magic that you managed to do all on your own!"

It was as if all the fatigue had been washed away from the four newly awakened girls as they all started talking over each other. About the man down in the village who had refused to believe them. About the shadow seekers that they had managed to chase away. About the Light Ceremony and how they had performed it. The cracks that had closed just in time.

"Excellent, Soul Riders," Avalon said, nodding contentedly. "Fantastic! Well done. I was afraid that it was too late," he said, looking out over the fire. "But you did it. You created the light seal and closed the cracks from Pandoria. I don't know how we're ever going to thank you."

"Thank us?" Lisa said, shrugging her shoulders. "It's kind of our job, isn't it?"

Linda thought Lisa sounded a little curt and remembered what she had said before. *What have the druids done to help us?* Avalon looked so happy. His face beamed with gratitude. Surely they could trust him, couldn't they?

"Where are you off to, by the way?" Lisa wondered, then added quickly, "I mean, I assume you must be on your way somewhere." She didn't want it to sound like she was trying to get rid of him. He might get suspicious.

"I set up camp a little way from here, just over there." Avalon shone his lantern toward a dense area of spruce trees. On the other side of the trees, they could make out a small, square clearing. "I thought we could ride to the Secret Stone Circle first thing tomorrow. Fripp and the other druids are waiting for you. We have so much to cover."

"Okay," Lisa responded. "That sounds good." But her heart was saying something totally different. It was saying, *No way.*

Linda glanced in Lisa's direction. Then she nodded. After running around putting out fires, it might be nice to go back to the Secret Stone Circle, Linda thought.

"Oh, by the way, Avalon?" she said, carefully taking the Light Ceremony book out of her saddle bag. "Could you take this now? So I don't need to feel responsible for it? It's kind of stressing me out, carrying the world's most important book around."

"Of course," Avalon said with a smile, stuffing the book into his pack. "But I'm going to let you girls rest now. You must be exhausted after this day. I'll see you first thing tomorrow!"

The girls crawled back into their sleeping bags.

Just before Linda fell asleep, she looked up at the sky and saw a new, and yet still familiar, constellation up there. It was in the shape of a moon, and it twinkled at Linda as if they shared a secret.

Linda winked at it. Then she closed her eyes and fell asleep.

Overnight, the temperature dropped down close to freezing for the first time that fall. The raw, damp chill penetrated the girls' sleeping bags, making everything feel cold and wet. Lisa woke up with her teeth chattering in the middle of a dream that slipped tantalizingly away from her. She sat up, shivering from the cold. Linda tossed her an extra blanket.

"Thanks," she mumbled, wrapping the blanket around herself.

"Were you able to get any sleep?" Linda wondered with a yawn.

"I think so," Lisa replied. "Strangely enough. I was pretty tired, I guess."

"Same here. I slept like a log," Anne said. She walked off to give the horses their breakfast.

"You were screaming in your sleep," Linda said, her eyes narrowing. "Did you know that?"

"Whoa, really?" Lisa blushed even though she didn't really know why. They didn't have any secrets from each other anymore, did they? She blew on her hands, scooted closer to the crackling fire that Linda had gotten going again. "I bet it was something about my dad," she said. "I'm so worried about him. Thank you for agreeing to ride there with me now," she added, boxing Linda gently on the arm.

"Uh, what? I thought we were going with Avalon to the Secret Stone Circle," Alex mumbled, tightening Tin-Can's girth. "That's what it sounded like last night anyway." Then she hoisted the saddlebags into position with a demonstrative thump. She didn't look in Lisa's direction.

"No," Lisa shook her head. "We're not. I will never let the druids stop me from rescuing my father. We're leaving now, and you're coming with me. Just like we decided yesterday before Avalon showed up. Who's with me?"

"You make it sound as if everything has already been decided," Linda objected. "I thought we made our decisions together."

"And I thought we helped each other," Lisa mumbled. "Sorry," she added quickly when she saw the sad look on Linda's face. "We can stand here pretending we're on the debate team if you want, but I'm planning to go get my dad no matter what. And, of course, I really want you guys to come with me."

"But then what about Avalon? Should we just leave him here in the woods?" Anne stopped grooming Concorde and turned around.

"Oh, we'll let him sleep," Lisa said. "The Secret Stone Circle has been there for thousands of years. It'll still be there after we rescue my dad."

Alex paced back and forth over the frosty ground. She sat down and ripped up a thick layer of moss. She avoided making eye contact with Lisa.

"Alex, I only have one parent who's still alive," Lisa whispered. Her eyes were full of tears. Something softened in Alex when she saw Lisa crying, but she wasn't planning to let it show. Not yet, anyway.

"My dad," Lisa continued. She was speaking more loudly now, more emphatically. "And I'm going to do whatever it takes to help him," she added. "The Secret Stone Circle can wait, like I said. Since we saved the dam, the druids and Fripp should be willing to give us a bit of a break."

With that, Lisa hopped up onto Starshine and started to ride away.

Alex mounted Tin-Can and as soon as she was settled in the saddle, she set out after Lisa.

"You want to catch up, old man?" Alex joked softly to her horse. She slowed down to keep pace with Lisa as soon as they caught up to her and Starshine. "Do you really think that this is a good idea, Lisa? You know how the rest of us feel about this. We're not so sure. But if you say so, if you really want to do this, we'll follow you."

Behind them, Meteor and Concorde pricked up their ears and broke into a trot as well.

Lisa heard Alex's words echoing in her head. She felt like she had a cold lump in her stomach. She didn't want to admit it, not even to herself, but she couldn't help but wonder if Alex was right. What if all of this was yet another huge mistake?

Her hands trembling, she pulled a well-worn picture out of her jacket pocket. It was faded from the sun and a little worn around the edges. It was a picture of her mother and father outside of their old house in Texas. The sun was shining in the bright blue sky and Lisa's father was shading his face with his hand. Lisa's mother was wearing a big cowboy hat and a plaid shirt. She was beaming.

Now only Lisa and her father were left. He was all she had. It didn't matter how dangerous it was or what the others thought. She *was* riding to Dark Core—and she *was* rescuing her father. He had waited long enough.

*But how?* a shrill, insistent voice whispered in her subconscious.

*I don't care how. I'll do anything.* She tightened her grip on the reins and urged Starshine forward.

*Don't be frightened, Dad. I'm coming soon.*

# 13

The closer they got to the ocean, the stronger the winds were. As they finally approached Dark Core Headquarters, the wind was blowing so hard it brought tears to their eyes. Their hair whipped in their faces, and they brushed it away with chapped hands and aching arms. They had ridden all day. It was already afternoon now, and the long ride was beginning to take its toll. Their legs were shaking from cold and exertion. The horses' heads were hanging, their pace slower and slower.

"We should have brought more clothes with us," Anne muttered. "I forgot how cold it gets along the coast this time of year."

"I wonder if it's this cold where my father is," Lisa said quietly.

"We'll know soon," Anne replied just as quietly. They smiled bravely at each other, but Lisa couldn't shake the icy lump in her stomach. What would happen when they made it into Dark Core?

*If they made it into Dark Core.* There was that skeptical voice again. Lisa wished it would drown in the ocean's choppy surf and be carried away by some of the crying seagulls swooping through the air above them. Even though it was still daytime, it felt like the sun was setting. The clouds were heavy and tinged with gray across the vast sky and dropped down to meet the ocean at the horizon. The contours of a gigantic oil platform came into view, looming menacingly in the distance. In front of the platform and the long bridge, they saw an equally large, greenish building of corrugated sheet metal.

"Do you see that?" Linda yelled between gusts of biting wind. "That's the old shipyard! That's where we're going!"

A plume of white smoke floated up from a chimney and out by the platform. Otherwise, everything was still. A row of vans with the unmistakable Dark Core logo on them were parked in front of the shipyard. The empty vehicles were the only sign that anyone was there. They couldn't hear any voices, footsteps, or sounds of work being done.

"It's too quiet," Alex muttered. "Too still. There's something shady about all this."

"Yeah, yeah," Lisa sighed. "Well, we'll see."

She didn't want to have this discussion with Alex again. Alex had come with her. That was all that mattered right now. They could deal with the rest later.

Lisa knew that getting into the headquarters would be no joke. Her father had described the whole procedure to her. First you had to go through the old shipyard, where one of the oil platforms was moored for repairs. Apparently, it had collided with an iceberg—at least that's what people said.

Cut through the shipyard, and then out onto the narrow bridge that they could just make out on the water. And then ride across the bridge to reach the actual oil platform. What awaited them there? Lisa remembered the men dressed in green at the Dark Core laboratory when she rescued Starshine, the flashlights that had blinded her, the roar of their engines, the feeling of being surrounded, helpless.

Her friends had gotten her and Starshine out of there. Would they be able to do that one more time? Lisa took a deep breath, trying to gather her thoughts, but it was no use. So many things suddenly became clear all at once. She realized that they didn't have a plan and that she didn't even know where her father was being held. Everything she did now, she realized she would have to do blindly. They would need to improvise.

The bracing onshore wind sent waves crashing against the bridge. The horses stopped and stood completely still in the wind with their ears flat, waiting.

"All right," Anne said, patting Concorde.

"It looks totally abandoned," Lisa said, swinging her hand out in way that she hoped seemed relatively confident. "Not a soul. I vote that we just try to go in and don't use magic until we need to. What do you guys think?"

The seagulls called out in the sky. The light blue DC sign on the building blinked at them.

Suddenly Alex burst out laughing.

"What's so funny?" Lisa wondered, annoyed.

Alex kept laughing and waved her hands dismissively. "Sorry, but I couldn't help it. This is such an insane idea. We're just going to, like, walk in? Just stroll right in like we're at some all-you-can-eat buffet at Jarla Pizza? Great! Do you seriously not get that this is a trap?! It shouldn't be this quiet. Doesn't anybody *work* here?"

Lisa hopped off of Starshine and lifted the reins over his head so that she could lead him more easily. Then she turned her back to Alex and led her horse through the open door into Dark Core Headquarters. She let the darkness and the uncertainty engulf her.

The others stared after her for a short time. Then, they followed her.

A good while later, the girls stood at the end of the long bridge, just outside of Dark Core's headquarters, where Lisa's father had spent many hours, first as an employee and then as a prisoner.

*You saw something you weren't supposed to see, Dad, so they took you,* Lisa thought. *But your captivity ends now. If everything goes the way it needs to, you will never see this building again. We're going to rescue you. Everything will go back to normal. Or at least as normal as our lives can be after all of this.*

They looked around. There were no workers dressed in green. The bright spotlights gave them long shadows as they hurried toward the entrance of the building.

"You stay here and stand guard, okay?" Linda asked, kissing Meteor on the nose.

Meteor shook his shiny brown head, scraped the ground with his hoof, and gave a high-pitched whinny.

"Shh," Linda whispered, stroking his forehead. "Not a sound from you."

Meteor shook himself again. Then, he pulled free of Linda's loose hold on his reins and trotted inside, right through the open doors. Starshine followed him, and then Concorde. Then, after having given Alex a look that seemed almost apologetic, Tin-Can reared up and trotted in, too. Alex shrugged and ran after him. Inside, the building was so much bigger than they could have imagined. The horses had plenty of room in the long, empty, echoing corridors. The girls followed the horses deeper into the building. They ran through the corridors as quickly as they could, their mouths dry and their lungs aching. The steady, rhythmic sound of the horses' hooves ahead of them gave them strength.

They ran until Lisa realized that Starshine had come to a sudden stop. He stood motionless, his ears pricked. Every muscle in his body seemed to be on alert.

"Starshine?" Lisa whispered. "What is it?"

The horse gave a soft snort. Then, he bent his head to the right, toward a barred door, and trotted over to it. Lisa followed Starshine. Seconds later, she screamed. Her friends looked over at her. Was she laughing? Or was she crying? Or maybe both at the same time?

Lisa had come to an abrupt stop right in front of the door and stood there staring. Inside, scarcely visible in the deep shadows, sat her father. It really *was* him!

"Dad!" Lisa whispered. "It's okay. We're here now."

She saw a beard and a pair of eyes floating in the darkness, then a string of white teeth with a glimmer of gold when her father smiled at her. Her father's gold tooth that she had been embarrassed about when she was younger. Now that gold tooth was the most beautiful sight she'd ever seen.

"Isa," he said hoarsely. "You came. I knew you would come!"

Anne's eyes filled with tears. She hastily wiped her cheek. Linda was also fighting back tears as she pointed mutely to the lock on the outside of the door. A key ring hung there, just waiting to be turned.

It was almost too good to be true. It *was* too good to be true, Lisa thought. Of course it was. But that didn't matter. Nothing else mattered, because she had finally found her father.

His eyes gleamed in the dark cell.

"We *need* to hurry now!" Alex hissed. "Because if this isn't a trap, then my name is John Sands."

Lisa turned the key in the lock with trembling hands. The door opened with a soft creak. Her heart felt like it was going to jump out of her chest. She practically flew to him, rushing into the cell and flinging her arms around her father's neck.

# 14

Lisa's dad was thinner than when she had last seen him, and so dirty that she couldn't help wrinkling her nose when she smelled the sour blend of dirt and old sweat. As he slowly got to his feet and stumbled toward her, he moved like an old man, not like the strong father she knew and loved. But she couldn't stop hugging him. He was her father and she was there.

She was finally there.

Lisa had a lump in her throat. She had to gulp several times to keep herself from crying.

"Come on," Lisa said, supporting her father under his arms. "We're going to help you out of here."

She shrank back when she saw the look in his eyes. His eyes moved dully and unfocused, past her and the other girls to the horses who stood completely motionless just outside the cell. She knew that the memories of the outings they had gone on when Lisa was little were still there. Somewhere inside her father, the warm prairie winds and the bluebells in the spring, the pine forests and fjords, the hot chocolate and cheese sandwiches, all of the stages of Lisa's life from when she was a baby until now, a whole lifetime remained. She realized that there must be so much more about her father's life that she had no idea about.

But right now, her father's eyes were just blank and empty. It made her heart feel heavy and sad.

"How are you doing, Dad?" Lisa whispered into his ear. "What did they do to you?"

"Isa . . ." he said weakly. Nothing more.

Lisa put her hand on her father's arm, frantically blinking back tears, calling on the stars. Maybe she could heal him, make him feel better?

But her father had already stood up and staggered out of the open cell door. Slowly, he made his way forward. Not back toward the main entrance, as Lisa expected, but out onto the big oil platform. They followed behind him. Lisa figured that her father knew his way around. He must know a way out.

*As long as he's aware of what he's doing.* Lisa thought back to the empty look that he had filled his eyes when she found him. She leaned against Starshine's warm coat. Her heart was pounding hard.

They were outside now, on the oil rig, completely unprotected from the ocean and the wind. The raw cold and the sea spray seeped into their clothes. But farther out on the platform, steam was forming, like when hot and cold come together. A faint glow reflected from the black water. Lisa's father was staggering toward the glow.

"No, Dad!" Lisa yelled. "The other way! We have to get out of here! Now!"

But Lisa's father kept going, out toward the round surface of the platform. He moved as if he was in a trance. Lisa rushed after her father, tugging on his arm, letting Starshine run free behind her.

"Dad?" Lisa yelled. "Come here!"

Then, she stopped abruptly. Because something rose up, towering in front of them. At first, Lisa thought that it was just a large, round statue. There weren't really any words to describe the strange structure, which was at least several yards tall and wide. But the strange mechanical arms and the wheel-like sides made of stone paled next to the bright fire that crackled and sparked in the middle of the device. Its flames flared up as the girls and their horses approached, as if their presence fed the fire.

Lisa instinctively backed away, uncomfortable as she watched the fire gain strength, growing from a faint glow to big, biting flames.

Tin-Can reared up on his hind legs. His hooves slammed against the hard surface of the platform. Alex lost hold of the reins and watched helplessly as her horse bolted away from her, closer to the flames, closer to the strange machine.

It was impossible not to look at the fire.

It was drawing them in now, luring them closer.

"Tin-Can!" Alex screamed into the wind. "Come back, pal!"

Linda fell down onto the platform as Meteor broke away and followed Tin-Can. Then Starshine followed and so did Concorde. The four horses galloped around in a frenzy. They stopped near the machine. Lisa's father rushed forward, with Lisa close on his heels. Starshine kicked to the rear and then rushed forward toward the machine, his hooves clattering against the hard metal surface. They were so close now that they could feel the cold, which seemed to seep into them. The fire wasn't giving off any heat, Lisa realized. What kind of fire makes a person feel ice-cold?

A creaking noise came from behind the device and a tall shadow fell over the ground. Lisa gasped, wanting to flee, but it was too late.

John Sands stepped out of the shadows and held out his scrawny, spider-like hands in an eerie, cheerful greeting.

## 15

John Sands took a step forward and bowed slightly, trium-phantly. His eyes looked almost red in the firelight.

"Ah, here you are! Welcome, we've been waiting for you!" he said with a smile.

Alex lunged at the pale, sickly looking man. Oh, how she wished she could zap that odious smirk right off his face! His gray trench coat hung loose at his sides, flapping in the wind. That, along with his unnaturally skinny limbs, made him look like an old scarecrow. And the horses reacted to him immediately, just like the birds at Scarecrow Hill, with visible fear. Tin-Can showed his long, yellow teeth and made a muffled sound that seemed to come from deep within his throat. It sounded almost like a growl. When Alex saw her brave horse like that—savage and scared out of his wits—it filled her with a red-hot hatred toward the man standing before her. She turned to Tin-Can and put a protective hand on his withers.

"There, there, boy. Easy does it." Alex looked Tin-Can right in the eye, and a warmth spread through her chest in spite of the icy chill from the machine's fire. A familiar lightning-flash sensation took over her. She raised her hand.

Anne stood beside her, her legs placed widely apart, communi-cating with Concorde without using any words. A vague flicker of light encircled them.

Lisa looked at Starshine, although she remained intensely aware of Mr. Sands's stifling presence the whole time. She hummed, so softly that only she could hear it, summoning the stars. Her voice shook a bit, but she kept going.

When Linda looked into Meteor's frightened eyes, she caught a glimpse of a moon. She blinked slowly, feeling the moon magic grow within her. Then she smiled encouragingly at her horse, who snorted softly. The look in his eyes mellowed and Linda knew that he understood. As long as they maintained eye contact, nothing dangerous could happen. As long as they acted as one, they were strong.

That's what she told herself, anyway.

Lisa's dad, Carl, stood perfectly still, looking from Mr. Sands to the Soul Riders and their horses. He looked as if he was about to pass out.

"Dad?" Lisa said, putting her hand on his shoulder. For a brief instant, she lost track of Starshine and the others.

A second later, Mr. Sands was standing right in front of them, so close that Lisa could smell his aftershave, citrus and something sharp, bitter. She already knew that if she ever smelled that scent again, she would throw up on the spot.

John Sands looked toward Lisa and her father with a faint smile on his lips.

*"Dad,"* he mimicked in a grotesque, squeaky voice, which Lisa assumed was meant to sound like her own. "Daddy. Papa Carl. Oh, to think that you and your friends rode here to rescue him! Very well done, Lisa. Admirable, actually." He took another step closer to her. "I know how it feels to want to fight for what you love. At one time I, too, had someone to love. Her name was Rosalinda. I tried to rescue her. I rescued her over and over again, but I didn't succeed. In the end I lost her, just as you are going to

lose your father. You understand, my little friend, unconditional love never ends well."

"Don't listen to him, Isa!" Her father's voice was quiet but clear. "He doesn't know what he's talking about!"

"Oh really, is that a fact?" John Sands cocked his head to the side and watched Carl carefully. But then his eyes darkened. "Believe me," he continued, "I know what I'm talking about. Enough chitchat now. Time to get to work."

Starshine whinnied sharply. *As a warning?* Lisa wondered. She pulled her hand back from her father's shoulder. She gulped and tried to return to the power of the stars, to the glances of safety exchanged between herself, her horse, and her friends. But she couldn't quite get back to it. She couldn't hear the music inside of herself anymore.

"As you must have figured out by now, we need your horses," Mr. Sands said. "Or to be more precise, their energy. That's an absolute requirement for the portal to work. Oh yes, and by the way, what do you think about my little device?" he added smoothly, nodding to the giant machine. "Impressive, isn't it?"

He continued talking in his same creepy tone. It almost made it seem like they were good, old friends, he was so relaxed and playful.

"Yes, now you've delivered the horses here," he smiled. "What good little Soul Riders you are. So gullible. It's wonderful to see. So maybe this would be a good time for me to say thank you? Or, what do you say, generals?"

The shadows seemed to gather over the dimly lit platform. Sabine stepped forward. Jessica appeared in the darkness behind her, and finally, a figure dressed in white appeared behind Jessica. Katja.

Alex swore quietly to herself. *We are so screwed. I predicted this. The trap of traps. And now it's too late.*

"We're ready," Sabine replied. The other two generals nodded.

A sucking, black void rose out of the portal and landed in Mr. Sands's hand. It looked like a small mass of dark, viscous clouds. The clouds grew thicker around the horses, who reared in frenzied panic.

Mr. Sands's voice was muffled and hoarse as he said, "Make way for Garnok! It's almost time!"

He raised his hand, and a thick, dark smoke floated upward. It changed shape as it hovered in the air, becoming rather snake-like and twisty.

Suddenly, it was hard to breathe, and the air around them felt weird, off somehow. Starshine staggered backward. Lisa tried to pull him toward her. She gathered her friends together, pushing them into a circle just like during the Light Ceremony. What was happening now? Whatever Mr. Sands and the Dark Riders were planning was also some kind of ceremony. That much she understood. Although the Light Ceremony had been about light and hope, this one was clearly an evil ceremony, one that sought to choke out light and extinguish hope altogether.

She squeezed Alex's hand. It felt cold and clammy in her own. Lisa opened her mouth, but no sound came out. Everything was muted. She felt like her whole body was going numb.

*What's going on?*

Katja's eyes gleamed white in the darkness. It looked like she was smiling.

Meteor brayed loudly, for a long time. Linda let go of Anne's hand in an effort to calm her horse, but she couldn't get to him. A cold loneliness spread through Linda. It began as an awful, numbing sensation in her fingers and spread to her brain, which also felt deadened. Her limbs wouldn't move. She mimed helplessly, hoping that someone would see what she was trying to say, but an icky black mist had settled around them. It stung their eyes.

Something flickered inside the machine. Mr. Sands reached his hand out toward the flames, so close that he should have wanted to recoil from the icy flames. But he didn't cringe; a cool smile rested on his thin, wrinkled lips.

A sharp thunderclap made Anne scream out loud. She couldn't tell if the sound had come from the sky or from the portal. She knew she should resist, do something, anything, but it was so hard to think. It was even harder to breathe. She couldn't remember what she was doing there, how she had gotten there. The dark clouds absorbed everything. She peered helplessly at Linda, who stood beside her, wishing that she could nod, blink, whistle, or scream, anything. But her friend looked just as helpless as Anne felt. Trapped in her own body.

As if through a fog, Linda remembered the first time she had discovered her magic, how everything had tingled, felt heightened, and also seemed bigger than in real life.

The magic that bubbled out of Mr. Sands's skeleton-like hands was the exact opposite. It leached away everything that was good, all that was life. She could see what was happening in Anne's blank face, in Lisa's screaming, expressionless look. She even saw it in Alex—*Alex*—who stood silent and still like a wax figure. The stronger the flames burned in the portal, the weaker they became. They tried multiple times, but their powers wouldn't come to them.

Time stretched and grew sticky. Mr. Sands continued chant-ing into the flames. His smile was broader now. His eyes shone feverishly. The words coming out of his mouth were no longer intelligible.

Something contracted inside Linda, a sudden, wide-awake awareness of the dense, viscous mist. *This is the darkness. Everything that came before was just practice. This is it now. Darkness is descending and taking us with it.*

Lisa managed to take her father's hand. She squeezed it tight as everything went black. Time froze and she gasped for air. A muted creaking sound came from inside the machine.

The three Dark Riders stood behind Mr. Sands. When Katja raised her hand, the creaking intensified. Lisa understood now that the Dark Riders were like conductors of evil. They were controlling the energy that Mr. Sands created from the portal, giving it air and oxygen.

It suddenly became even harder to breathe. Lisa looked helplessly at Starshine, trying to make eye contact, thinking, *It's now or never, pal. Can you help me? Please?*

An electric shock ran through Lisa as Starshine made eye contact with her. For a fraction of a second, she could no longer see the platform. She couldn't see Mr. Sands or the Dark Riders. No fire, no blackness, no toxic smoke. She saw only her horse, and the stars that shone in his eyes.

It happened quickly after that. Starshine turned to Concorde and whinnied shrilly. The big horse whinnied back, even louder, got ready, and then reared.

Then an airy, almost crisp sound could be heard across the platform. Something swished toward them, and fast. Anne's mouth fell open when she saw it. Concorde went soaring toward Mr. Sands and the Dark Riders. Just like that: soaring, because two massive white wings had taken shape on his glistening gray sides. Anne felt her legs give way. Suddenly she remembered a picture that she had seen in an old book once. A winged horse that looked exactly like Concorde. The little hairs on the back of her neck stood up as she saw the wings beating against Mr. Sands's face, causing him to lose his balance. At that moment, the platform was lit up by a light so bright that it blinded them all.

With a roar that set their teeth on edge, Mr. Sands lost his balance and fell into the fire.

A hissing sound slid over Sabine's lips. She lunged for the portal, for Mr. Sands. Along with Katja and Jessica, she flung herself forward and pulled at Mr. Sands's trench coat, trying to pull him back up, out of the portal. That was the last thing that the Soul Riders saw before a deafening bang, followed by a hoarse screeching sound, made them drop to the ground covering their heads with their hands.

When they dared to look again, Mr. Sands was gone, swallowed up by the portal. A dull, black liquid exploded with a sizzle over the platform. It was like an oil bath of hot, bubbling dark magic.

The Dark Riders convulsed, flung themselves around. Enormous flashes of lightning shook the machine. Sabine fell headfirst into the shiny black water below the platform. Yet another resounding bang. Katja and Jessica tumbled in after her. The waves splashed against the railings. For a brief instant, echoes could be heard of a frantic roaring from the bottom of the ocean, distant but urgent.

Then everything went quiet.

# 16

Slowly, the four Soul Riders got back up again, looking around in disbelief. The machine seemed to have shut off. Mr. Sands was gone. But where did he go? And where were the Dark Riders? One by one, the girls ran over to peer down into the glistening black ocean. Linda's heart was pounding inside her rib cage as she leaned forward. What would she do if she saw a pale face staring back up at her? But where the water had just been swelling around the Dark Riders when they fell, the surface was now smooth and dark. There was only a faint hint of a ripple.

Alex hurried over to the portal. She put her trembling hands on it.

"Alex, no!" Linda yelled. "We don't know if it's safe!"

"I just have to check," Alex responded. "That weird electricity and smoke that zapped us all . . . I just have to make sure that it's completely gone before we get out of here."

She waited to see if she felt anything, a charge, a sign. But everything was cool and calm. There were no longer any embers inside the portal. Alex shook her head.

"I . . . that . . ." Alex said, shaking her head in irritation when she couldn't think of the right words.

"I know," Linda said, walking over to Meteor. He flattened his ears and backed away. Linda looked concerned. "What is it,

Meteor? Are you afraid he's going to come back? He's gone now." To herself, she thought, *For the moment, anyway*. But she didn't want to say that out loud.

"Thanks to Concorde," Anne said, patting her horse. He, too, backed away from her touch. *Weird*.

Lisa walked over to Starshine, but her feet felt big and awkward, as if she were wearing oversized clown shoes. She stroked Starshine's forehead, waiting for the feeling of warmth, the one that always filled her when she approached her horse.

*Nothing*. She felt only empty and hollow. Even so, she smiled a big, hard-won smile when she turned to her father and said, "Dad, you get to ride Starshine now. He's going to bring us home. I'll walk along beside you and lead him."

"Hi, Starshine. What a beautiful horse you are," Lisa's dad said and carefully ran his hand over the bright white bridge of the horse's nose. Starshine stood still, letting himself be pet. Starshine's eyes were just as vacant as Lisa's father's eyes had been just a few minutes earlier.

"You're tired, pretty boy," Lisa whispered into Starshine's ear. "We'll all get a chance to rest. Soon."

*Yes*, Lisa thought. *The horses just need to rest a little*. That was all. Then, once this awful explosion was behind them, everything would go back to normal.

Everything would be all right. She repeated that to herself, whispering it quietly into Starshine's coat, which still smelled like the stables and home even though it had been a while since they were last there. She helped her father up onto Starshine's back and then led him out through the gates. It felt like the calm after a storm. Everything was deserted and quiet.

It was starting to get dark for real now, but the sky was lit with a pinkish glow that made Anne feel uneasy. Once they were off of the platform, they heard a loud thud. She jumped, took a breath, and said, "He disappeared into that—into that strange machine? Into the portal, didn't he?"

"I don't know where he went, but I don't think he can hurt us anymore," Linda said with a nod.

"And Sabine and the others?"

"Well, we saw them vanish into the water." Now Linda sounded less sure. "I think . . . I hope . . ." She paused, her eyes sweeping over the water. Was it just her imagination or did she see a figure out there? Something dark and shiny, swimming toward shore, smoothly and purposefully? It could be a seal. But unfortunately, Linda knew that wasn't what it was. The Dark Riders seemed to escape every time.

But she didn't have any strength left to investigate, and she knew that none of the others did either. So, with one last look back over her shoulder, she rode to catch up with them, leaving the oil platform behind her.

The oil platform stood quietly in the dark when its motion detectors suddenly went off. A wet figure laboriously climbed up onto it. Her long braid dripped ice-cold ocean water. She spat and sputtered, cursed the ocean and what was hidden under those surging waves.

"Hurry up, you guys!" Sabine hissed. "I'm freezing to death."

"Oh please, you know you can't freeze to death." Katja's voice was gentle, almost soft. She looked annoyingly blasé, Sabine thought, as she climbed up onto the rig, as lithe as a cat. When Katja's chalk-white hair was slicked back by the water, you could make out the contours of her skull underneath. The skin on her face was bluish and thin.

"Sands seems to be gone, at least," Jessica said, once she succeeded in making her way up onto the platform. Her blue eyes casually scanned the quiet machine. "What do we do now?"

"Await Garnok's wrath," Sabine replied sourly. "Unless you have some exciting new hobby you want to take up."

"Garnok is still close," Katja said. "After all, everything went according to plan. The Soul Riders and their horses are broken, their energy drained. Although they won't realize that until it's too late."

Sabine smiled quickly at Katja in response before she turned around and started to jog toward the bridge where Khaan stood waiting.

# 17

The four Soul Riders rode slowly through the cold evening. Night was almost upon them. Normally, they would alternate between trotting and cantering with short walking breaks in between, but now, for Lisa's father's sake, they were walking the whole way home. Lisa walked alongside Starshine, leading him.

"He's never been on a horse before," Lisa said when Alex and Linda sighed impatiently. "We need to be careful."

"How is it even possible to live on a ranch in Texas without learning to ride a horse?!" Linda whispered in Lisa's direction.

"I managed the grounds crew," Carl responded with a weak smile. Then he closed his eyes and nodded off in the saddle.

"Fine, you guys walk, but I'm going to ride ahead. I can't deal with this snail's pace," Alex announced, and then pressed Tin-Can on. For a moment, he started a leisurely trot, but quickly slowed. Annoyed, Alex urged him on again. "Come on, pal!"

Tin-Can tossed his head and flattened his ears. After that he stopped abruptly and started backing up instead of walking forward. Alex leaned down to pat his neck.

"Hey, buddy, what's the matter with you? Don't you want to go home?"

"He's probably tired," Anne responded. "Like we all are."

With a deep sigh, Alex gave Tin-Can free rein to walk at a slow, leisurely pace. He immediately stopped his monkeying around, and they rode on. A flock of seagulls circled in the night sky. Everything else was quiet.

"I think there's something wrong with the horses," Alex said after a long time. "Something happened on the platform. I told you guys we shouldn't ride there!"

"They're just tired. That's all," Lisa retorted quickly. Maybe too quickly. Her father opened his eyes and looked at her. Even though he was so quiet, having him close made her feel safe. "Rest now, Dad," she said. "We'll be home soon."

A few hours later, the exhausted group dropped off their horses at Jorvik Stables. Herman came out and eagerly met them in the stable yard.

"You're back!" he declared, beaming with joy. "Finally! I could hardly believe my ears when you called, Lisa," he added, smiling warmly at her. "And you brought Starshine and Concorde! Wonderful! And . . . who's this?" He looked on curiously as Carl awkwardly clambered down off of Starshine's back.

"Herman, this is my father, Carl," Lisa replied. "Dad, this is Herman, whom I've told you so much about."

Herman held out his big hand and enthusiastically pumped Carl's hand up and down. If he noticed that Carl was dirty and his clothes ragged, he didn't say anything.

"Nice to meet you, Carl," Herman said and then turned to Lisa. "Well, I've already heard about your accomplishments. We're proud of you, girls. And by *we*, I mean myself and our friends up in the mountains." He winked knowingly at Lisa so that she would understand that he was referring to the druids.

"They wanted me to tell you to get some rest now and await further instructions. As soon as we know more about the situation, I'll let you know," Herman said. "You'll be needing your strength soon, so rest up as much as you can. You deserve it after all you've been through. I'll update those who need to know."

"And Elizabeth?" Alex said eagerly, her pulse speeding up. Maybe she could still dare to hope after all . . . ?

Herman looked down and shook his head.

"No good news there, unfortunately," Herman said. "And with every day that goes by, the chances of her being brought back decrease . . ."

Alex's eyes filled with tears. Herman put his big hand on her shoulder and said, "I suggest that you guys get the horses into the stables on the double. Then pile into my car and I'll give you all a ride home. Like I said, you need your rest now, all of you."

Starshine flattened his ears back and whined at Lisa as she brought him back to his stall and started to remove his girth. She stroked his neck carefully. "Not in the mood, sweetheart? You know I understand, right? I totally get it."

Normally, she would have stayed with Starshine for a while. She would pet him, maybe even sing to him a little. She knew it was a little dorky to sing to a horse, but he seemed to like it. Besides, he wasn't like the other horses. As if she needed to remember that after everything that they had just experienced . . .

*But even super horses needed rest after something like that,* she thought as she shut the door to his stall.

When she came out of the stable, she saw her father standing by the car, talking to Herman. He looked pale and tired, but he was listening attentively, even chuckling now and then when Herman apparently said something funny.

Everything seemed normal—*almost normal,* at any rate. This was no ordinary moment in the stable, they all knew that. But if any outsider—a riding school student who had forgotten their helmet, for example—should come running in, everything would have looked pretty normal and unremarkable. Just two men, one older and one somewhat younger, standing and making small talk while they waited for the youngsters to finish with their horses.

An enormous wave of gratitude flooded over Lisa. She hurried out to the two men and gave her father a big hug. He returned it and smiled, a little surprised.

"I'm so glad you're here, Dad," she whispered.

"Glad to be here," he replied. "You have no idea."

"Yeah," she answered with the shadow of a smile. "I do." She looked into her father's eyes and saw they were wet with tears.

Herman stood quietly, watching them. Then, in a gentler voice than usual, he said, "What do you say I give you a ride home now? You must be dead tired."

Carl rubbed his eyes and coughed slightly.

"Dead tired sounds about right. Come on, girls." Carl ruffled Lisa's hair and followed Herman over to the car. "Time to go home and get some sleep."

The girls piled into the back seat. Lisa sat on Anne's lap, making a face every time her kneecaps hit the back of the driver's seat. She leaned against Alex, who was sitting next to Anne, and wrinkled up her nose.

"You really smell," Lisa said.

"I hate to say it, but you don't exactly smell like roses yourself," Alex responded with a wry smile.

Even though it was a tight fit, it was really cozy in the back seat of the car. Herman had the radio on a station that played '60s pop music and Lisa hummed along. She looked out the window, straight into the darkness, trying to fathom the fact that they were really there now, safe in the back of Herman's car, not at the dam trying to prevent a disaster from happening, not at Dark Core's oil platform with Mr. Sands and the Dark Riders. Suddenly all of that felt like a bad dream. Lisa couldn't understand how they had actually managed to pull it all off.

"You guys?" she said as Herman pulled onto her street. "You know what? We're the best."

"We know," Alex replied sleepily.

"Mhmm," Anne mumbled against her shoulder.

"Remind me about that tomorrow after I've had about thirteen hours of sleep, will you?" Linda said, and then yawned. But her eyes twinkled as she said it.

Their whole front yard was dotted with apples, Lisa noticed as she got out of the car and said goodbye. Shiny red and pale yellow, they lay in piles on the unkempt lawn. Some had already begun to rot. Lisa's bike was leaning against a cobweb-covered windowsill. The lights were off in all of the windows, which made the house look gloomy. Even so, her heart beat faster as she got out of the car with her father beside her.

*Home.*

Finally.

# 18

A few days later, Lisa was up in her room alone. There was a framed drawing in Lisa's bedroom, sitting on her desk, which was strewn with drawing supplies, schoolbooks, and a little wireless speaker. It was of a white horse with an electric blue mane. You could tell that a child had drawn it; the lines were clunky, the proportions a little off. The tail stood up like a blue feather, dancing in an invisible wind. The horse was alone and free, without a saddle or bridle, galloping on a green hillside.

A green and blue hillside, actually. Halfway through coloring it, the green marker had run out of ink, and Lisa had to use a bluish-green marker instead to finish it. While that color was perfect for drawing the ocean, it was less so for grass.

Lisa still remembered how angry she had felt when she saw how bad it looked, how close she had been to crumpling up the drawing and starting over. But her mother had picked it up from the table and told her that it was great and noted what a beautiful color the horse's mane was! Her mother had framed the drawing and kept it in her study.

Then, AFTERWARD, when her father was going through her mother's things, he asked if she would like to keep the picture. His eyes teared up as he held it.

Since then, it had gone everywhere with Lisa, from Texas to Alaska, all the way to Norway—and now to Jorvik. She probably should have swapped out the frame, she thought, running her hand over the cracked glass. But she just couldn't bring herself to do it. Somehow the cracks in the glass went with the childish lines of the drawing. It should be a little worn, a little flawed. It should show that she had lived with that drawing for her whole life, through tears and loss.

Lisa preferred things a little worn and used. She essentially lived in her mother's old leather jacket now. By this point, it was just as soft and supple as a second skin. Her favorite thing to do on a Saturday was to visit the secondhand record shop in Jarlaheim and look for old vinyl records that she could play on her record player. At one time, the record player had belonged to her mother. Now that her mother could no longer play her favorite records, Lisa did it for her. The songs and dreams could live on even though her mother couldn't.

That horse in the drawing that Lisa had made when she was little had come to life. He existed. She knew that now. Even back then, so many miles away from Jorvik Stables, he had called to her through time and space. She had never talked to anyone about the special horse that she couldn't stop drawing. He had been her secret, just hers. The blue of his mane became deeper as the years went by. So did her longing for him.

And now? Now he was hers. *Hers!* Just like in a fairy tale. He was in his stall just a short bike ride away from her house. But Lisa wasn't planning to ride there, not today. Maybe not tomorrow, either. She kept running her finger over the cracked glass and felt the tears begin.

Starshine was so close—and yet so far away. Last night, when she had prepared him for an evening ride in the woods, she could tell right away that something was wrong. He didn't greet her as she walked down the aisle toward his stall. No soft snort, no gentle muzzle pushing into her hand as she opened the stall door. No warm sigh, no curious, pricked ears. Just . . . grayness. The music and the magic were gone. The colors, too. Had the world always been so gray?

*I don't care about being a Soul Rider*, Lisa thought as she stood leaning against her apathetic horse. *I don't even care about music. I could smash my guitar when I get home, jump on it and stomp on the splinters, build a bonfire out of it in the yard. I would do whatever it takes if I could only get Starshine back.*

It wasn't that long ago that she had believed she would never get to see him again. Now they were home and she had her Starshine back. So why did everything feel so wrong? Why didn't he want to gallop anymore? Starshine always loved speed.

Frustration had finally made her bang her legs too hard into Starshine's sides, like a confused beginner, when riding him. Nothing helped. Her hands were rigid. She could hardly feel Starshine underneath her, just a massive, horse-like lump that refused to obey. She turned back toward the stable with a numb grayness inside her. She quickly unsaddled Starshine. No grooming, no treat. No whispering of confidential secrets into his ear. There was nothing to say.

Her dream horse, her Starshine. He watched her as if she were a stranger. It hurt so much to think about. Through all of the strange things that had happened since she moved to Jorvik, she'd had Starshine's support. And now? What happened now?

Herman had been in touch and said that the druids could still feel the presence of John Sands and the Dark Riders. Magical forces were in motion, evil forces. Although none of the druids—no, not even Fripp, who could read the stars—knew exactly what was going to happen. Or when. So, they waited. It felt like their whole lives were on pause.

Waiting to hear more from the druids.

Waiting for news about Elizabeth.

Waiting for the horses to recover.

Waiting for . . . well, what? *Something.* Lisa could feel this *something* like a faint echo, an off note. She closed her eyes and tried to listen intently, but all she could hear was the hum of a car engine. That must be her father coming back from the grocery store. They were going to have spaghetti with Bolognese sauce tonight. She had promised her father she would help. *Chop a bunch of onions,* Lisa thought, and smiled grimly. *Great, then I can keep crying in peace and quiet for a while longer . . . without anyone taking notice.*

With a sigh, she set down the drawing and headed for the kitchen.

"Wow, that turned out great," her father said an hour later as they sat at the dinner table.

"Have some more," Lisa replied, pushing the pan closer to him. Her father saluted her and reached for the roasted carrots with sauce. "Aye aye, captain."

"Don't you mean *oh captain, my captain?*" Lisa replied with a fleeting smile, thinking of the movie that was both of their favorite, the one that they had watched together so many times. She wanted to watch it with her father again soon. *It's not weird to cry when you're watching a sad movie,* she thought. They're a little like onions, the perfect alibi for tears. You can let go of your inhibitions and just turn on the faucets. Nice. Although of course it would have been even better if she didn't need to cry at all.

Soon, maybe, Lisa hoped. Once Starshine was himself again.

And her father? Was he himself? She studied him attentively as he ate his food. In his T-shirt and favorite sweatpants, her father looked almost like his usual self. His cheeks were clean-shaven. His hair was combed, and he had styled it with some gel the way he did when he had to go somewhere, although his tired eyes made it clear that he didn't intend to leave the sofa tonight, either. He was still pale and worn out, and Lisa could hear him screaming in his sleep at night.

She wondered if his nightmares were anything like hers.

Lisa chased those thoughts away and sucked up a long strand of spaghetti. It splashed a little sauce onto her nose, which she wiped away. It was starting to get dark outside. She glanced out at the big oak tree outside the window. The enormous black branches were like shadowy figures against the bluish-black sky. A restless longing came over her.

Then her father said, "I've been doing some thinking over the last few days. There's something I want to discuss with you."

"Sure," Lisa replied. She stood up and cleared the plates. Her heart was racing. Was this going to be the big Soul Rider conversation? Her father must have a thousand questions after everything that had happened out on the platform.

But instead her father said, "I think we should move."

Lisa dropped the plates on the floor. The white porcelain shattered into little pieces as it hit the wood floor. She stood there, staring at the mess.

"Lisa?" Her father's voice sounded distant. "Did you hear what I said? I think we should move, leave Jorvik. This isn't a good place.

107

It's dangerous, and my job at the oil platform isn't keeping us here anymore."

Lisa sat back down at the table again, leaving the smashed plates on the floor where they fell.

"I heard you," she said. "And that's a big, fat no from me. Now that I have friends and I've met Starshine, I can never move! Mr. Sands is gone. You said so yourself. He can't hurt us anymore." She cleared her throat. "Hurt *you*, I mean. I am NOT moving."

Her father gave her a sad look.

"Okay," he sighed. "We'll continue this conversation another time. I'll wash up so you can head over to the stables."

"The stables? Now?" Lisa turned to him with a puzzled expression.

"Yes," he answered, "you probably want to go see Starshine and your friends, right?"

"Maybe tomorrow," she said with a shrug. "I have home-work to do."

Her father raised an eyebrow but didn't say anything. Lisa got up from the table and let the dark blue twilight mood sweep over her.

There was nowhere to go tonight. Only more of that weird emptiness waited at the stables, and what if the others were there? She didn't feel like talking to them yet. She didn't want to face the weird things that were happening with the horses, or her father's plan to move away from Jorvik. Better to stay home in her bed-room, where she could get lost in her music and try to forget about it all for a while.

She went to her room and closed the door, then took out her guitar and started to play. The framed drawing was still facedown on her desk. She was careful not to look at it.

· ✦ ·

Later, when she went downstairs to say goodnight to her father, she overheard him talking on the phone. He was practically
screaming as he paced back and forth. The broken plates had
been swept up.

"So, you're refusing to accept my police report? Totally unbeliev-
able! I'm not going to drop this!"

Lisa snuck back up the stairs before her father had a chance to
turn around and catch her eavesdropping.

# 19

"Come on, Meteor! One more time now! I know you can do it, buddy!"

Linda pushed her eyeglasses back up on her nose, shortened the stirrup straps, and then cantered one lap around the riding ring. Then, she moved into a forward seat and started riding toward the jump that Meteor had just knocked a rail off of.

It was a small jump, at least thirty-three centimeters lower than the oxers and triple bars that they usually sailed over in jumping competitions, pure child's play. This was a mere warm-up exercise before—as always—she raised the jump's height. Still, Meteor knocked it down. After first refusing to even attempt it at all several times. Her horse was definitely not in the mood, and she would have to cut the ride short soon. There didn't seem any point in continuing, she thought. Just one more time, one last time . . .

Linda looked determined as she rode toward the jump. She counted the strides and rallied Meteor a little. The yellow and green stripes of the rails gleamed in the soft fall twilight. She had helped to paint them only a few weeks earlier.

She thought back to when she felt it turned out really nicely. Now, she felt that the cheerful colors looked mockingly upbeat. Black would have been more fitting now.

With her line of sight fixed over the obstacle, she raised her hands just a smidge so that they were resting against Meteor's thick mane. She could already feel them flying over the jump together, even now. That delightful rush in the pit of her stomach. Jumping was the best thing in the world to Meteor. Linda had decided that she would only attempt jumps that were on the easy side for him today because he had been so tired over the past few days. Jumping usually perked him up. She knew it would help this time, too.

She smiled a little as she felt Meteor getting ready. *Easy, easy, you've got it now. Good boy, atta boy, Meteor!*

A second later he came to an abrupt stop in the middle of the jump and Linda flew out of the saddle and over the rails. Alone. She landed in the sand with a thump.

"Ow," she muttered, rubbing her tailbone. Meteor remained on the other side of the jump with the reins hanging around his neck, looking at her. His brown eyes were inscrutable.

"All right, thanks for that," Linda mumbled in annoyance. But she could never withstand that warm look from under his light, tangled forelock, and this was no exception. She threw her arms around her horse's neck and hugged him tight, inhaling the heavy scent of horse sweat into her nostrils.

"What is it, buddy? What's wrong?" she whispered.

A growing sense of concern filled her chest. There *was* something wrong, she knew that much. Meteor, the biggest pig in the whole stable, who was constantly coming up with new ways to sneak out of his stall at night to munch on hay, seemed to have lost his appetite. Linda had called the veterinarian the day before and she had come and examined him and taken some tests. She hadn't found anything. All the tests were perfect. The veterinarian explained that horses have bad days, too, just like people do.

Deep down inside, Linda suspected what was wrong. She pressed her face into his soft coat and thought of how she had hidden from Sabine inside Pine Hill Mansion. The darkness had already reached her then. It didn't matter how hard she tried to hide—Sabine had sunk her claws into her and made her weak. She had leached something out of her. Linda suspected that that was what Mr. Sands had done to Meteor now: sucked all of his energy out like a vampire. It wasn't exactly something she could tell the veterinarian, but she knew in her gut that it was true.

"My beloved Meteor," Linda whispered sadly. "What should we do?"

Linda wanted everyday life to return to normal. She wanted a life in which she didn't have to be on the run all the time, wracking her brain until she felt empty, fighting until she had nothing left. Oh, to just perch herself on the window ledge in her room with a bunch of cozy candles lit, a steaming cup of tea, and her cat Misty on her lap—how she missed that!

When they had been forced to sleep out in the damp, freezing forest with danger lurking everywhere, that had been practically the only thought that could comfort her. The thought of being home again soon. To be able to forget everything that had happened, even if just for a little while. To jump with Meteor, read books, go to school, spend time with her friends, record new videos of her cat, the luxury of just being normal.

"But we're not normal, you and me, are we?" Linda said tenderly to her horse. "That's the thing."

Meteor's head felt heavy and warm in her arms. She didn't know how long they had been standing like that, but suddenly she heard the sound of hooves approaching the paddock. She slowly let go of Meteor's neck and stretched, peering toward the stable, where the sound was coming from. She saw long blond hair and a graceful gray horse walking toward her. She grinned.

"Anne!" she yelled, waving.

Anne smiled back, leading Concorde into the paddock.

"Practicing jumps?" she said, tightening the girth, to Concorde's protest. He stamped restlessly back and forth and tossed his big, shimmering gray head.

"Mhmm, or that was the plan anyway," Linda replied, squirming slightly. "It didn't go so well today," she explained. "Meteor's not in the mood."

"I've got another one here who's not in the mood," Anne said sadly. "But I thought that a little exercise would probably do him good. It usually helps."

It was quiet for a moment. The two friends looked at each other's horses in the October evening twilight. A car engine started and faded away into the distance. They could hear muffled whinnying from the stables.

"It's not like it was before, is it?" Linda finally said. "You feel it, too, right?"

"Yeah," Anne said quietly. "I don't know what we should do."

Linda felt the evening's chill working its way into her quilted jacket. She felt like she wanted to go home now, take a long shower, and read in bed with Misty curled up next to her like a warm, purring ball of fur. And then she would come up with a solution. She would make sure that the horses could return to their normal selves again.

"We'll come up with something," Linda said. "We always do, don't we? On our own, or with Herman and the druids' help. Good luck with your ride. I'm going to head back in and try and get some dinner into Meteor before I go home."

Anne eyed Linda skeptically. Meteor was the biggest pig of a horse she'd ever known. That was a standing joke at the stable: *Hurry, before Meteor comes and eats up all of the oats in Jorvik.*

"Uh, what did you just say?" Anne asked.

"I know, right? He's not eating well at all," Linda replied, eyeing her horse with concern.

"If Meteor isn't eating, something must be *really* wrong," Anne said. A shadow fell over her face. Her eyes looked truly concerned. She sighed a little, then mounted Concorde and asked for a walk.

Before Linda turned around, she had a chance to see how the big gelding tossed his head in irritation. They moved fitfully through the evening darkness in the paddock, not at all as elegantly and smoothly as they usually did. Watching Anne ride Concorde was usually like watching a beautiful dance. It was almost impossible to tell where the horse ended and Anne began. They usually moved as one, in perfect harmony, but Linda didn't see any sign of that tonight. She saw only a frustrated rider struggling to get through to her horse.

*Yeah,* Linda thought as she led Meteor back to the stable. *Something is really wrong.* They would find a way to help the horses and make everything all right again, together, but how?

Something in the back of her mind was bothering her, like an old mosquito bite you thought had stopped itching. Somewhere deep down inside, something was trying to get out, a thought, a feeling . . . Linda stopped in the aisle in the middle of the stable. She closed her eyes, focusing, taking her time. The feeling slipped away and then everything was quiet again—far too quiet.

Nothing.

That was exactly what she wrote in her diary later that night. *Nothing.* She stared at the word for a long time. Seven completely worthless letters. She erased them and started over. Her arm twitched, but no new words came to her.

She brushed her teeth, looking her tired reflection straight in the eyes.

Nothing.

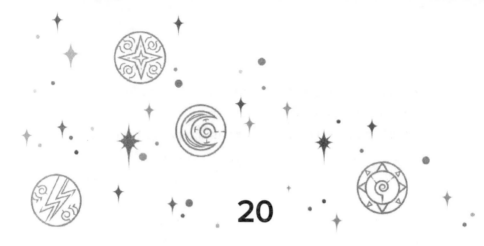

# 20

The spotlights around the outdoor riding ring, which were on timers, came on with a crackle. Suddenly the ring was bathed in sharp light. Anne rode diagonally through, changed directions, and sighed impatiently. She felt like she had been warming Concorde up for about half an eternity, working with voltes and exercises to loosen him up, trotting, and riding gently. It didn't usually take this much effort to get Concorde warmed up. He was sluggish and unfocused tonight. She had to fight to get his attention.

She could feel Concorde underneath her. As if through a fog, she could see his long legs trotting along when she looked down toward the ground. But their movements were out of step with each other. When she urged him to speed up, he slowed down, and when she tried to get him to slow to a walk, he sped up. Nothing she did seemed to help. She couldn't remember the last time she had ridden this badly.

Wait, yes, actually, she could. It was like this yesterday. And the day before that. It had been like this ever since they had returned from their fall break adventure. She just *couldn't* get Concorde to listen to her.

She used to look forward to every dressage session. Now she dreaded them. What used to be play had become a struggle.

How could this happen? She sighed again. Frustration tingled up and down her arms and legs.

*Luckily, no one is here to see this,* she thought, asking for a stop. That would have been so embarrassing. She wondered how much Linda had seen earlier. Annoyed, she pulled her feet out of the stirrups and dismounted.

"What's with you these days, sweetie?" she whispered, thoughtfully stroking the big gelding's neck. He responded by flattening his ears back and baring his teeth at her. Anne flinched. It felt like a punch in the face. Her eyes filled with tears and she gasped for breath.

*I thought we had something, you and me,* she thought as she led a resisting Concorde back to the stable. *Something special, a magical bond. I thought it was us against the world. I traveled through time and space to find you, my beloved horse. I was prepared to give up my life for you. Did I do something wrong? Is this my punishment?*

When Anne and Concorde entered the stable, they found Herman whistling cheerfully. He stopped abruptly when he saw the look on Anne's face.

"Tough night?" he asked empathetically.

"You could say that," Anne mumbled in response, leading her horse to his stall. He flattened his ears again as she untacked him. For the first time ever, she felt something akin to fear before grooming him.

Sure, Concorde had occasionally been a bit peevish in the past, but she had always known where she stood with him. She had always felt safe.

But now? Now her heart was racing, fast. Her adrenaline was pumping. She groomed him at arm's length, avoiding his head and rear legs. Her whole body was trembling.

*Would you look at me now?* she thought determinedly. *Raised in stables, with a whole bedroom full of awards and trophies, and I'm barely brave enough to brush my horse.*

Inside his stall, Meteor kicked the wall, loudly. That wasn't a grooming sound. Linda must have already gone home. That was a shame. It would have been nice to talk to her a bit more right now. Maybe they could have started trying to figure out what was wrong with the horses. Feeling sad, she ran her eyes over Concorde. He was standing only a few yards away from her, but he felt a world away. She would do anything to get through to him.

"Please," she whispered, starting to cry. "Please, Concorde, tell me what to do. I just want everything to go back to normal."

# 21

When her cell phone started to ring, Alex thought about not answering. She let it ring, echoing over the water and the rocks. Finally, right before her rock music ringtone faded away, she answered.

"Hi, Alex," Herman said. "I thought I would just call and see if you wanted to come and help out at the stables? Maybe move a few hay bales? No one does it as well as you, you know."

Alex felt a pang of guilt when she said, "I don't think I can today. Unfortunately, I have to study so I'll probably spend another night in Jorvik City."

"Okay." Herman sounded surprised, but he didn't say anything more. Alex put her phone back in her pocket, her cheeks burning. Why was it so hard to lie to Herman?

The coast spread out before her. The ocean was dark gray and wild tonight, splashing her sneakers whenever a wave broke on the rocky shoreline. Alex often came here when she needed to think. There was something about the salty air and the barrenness here that always managed to calm her down. Often, a few deep breaths of the ocean air were enough to ease whatever was weighing on her mind. It was nice to feel small and powerless compared to the rocks, the wind, and the massive ocean. It put everything into per-spective, made everything clearer. She liked being here at sunset, like now, best of all. She wouldn't leave until the ocean grew dark and glossy.

She liked to imagine that she was putting the ocean to bed. When Alex was little, she had to put herself to bed almost every night. She would lie there alone on her small cot in the closet, listening to her mother cry and shush her little siblings on the other side of the wall. When her mother yelled, *I can't take this!* and Alex heard how her mother's voice cracked, she thought of the waves rolling in from the ocean. When she closed her eyes, she could almost feel herself being rocked by those waves, softly and quietly. It wasn't the same as falling asleep in her mother's arms. It certainly wasn't. But since her mother never had time to put her to bed, the waves had to do it instead.

Now it was her turn to put the ocean to bed.

She usually brought Tin-Can here. But not today. She gulped, thinking about how tired he had looked the last time she'd seen him. Her high-spirited, mischievous boy. What if she'd done something to him? Ridden him to pieces, pushed him too hard. Her stomach hurt just thinking about it.

And yet . . . Tin-Can wasn't like other horses. He was a Starbreed, just like her friends' horses, and Starbreeds had extra everything—extra strength, extra endurance, extra intelligence.

After everything that had happened over the past few months, Alex was starting to understand that Starbreeds—just like Soul Riders—were magical in some ways. But you couldn't take the magic for granted. And yet that was just what she had done, she realized now as she looked out at the darkening ocean. She had exposed Tin-Can to danger by letting him come near Mr. Sands. Now he needed to rest so he could be himself again.

*If it's not already too late. We should never have ridden to Dark Core. If only I had stuck up for myself more . . .* She jumped as if someone had slapped her. Yeah, why hadn't she stood up for herself more? It wasn't like her to back down like that. Was it? She braced herself against the thought. Finally, it wedged its way back in anyway.

Was everything that Lisa had been saying actually true? Was there something wrong with her?

*Of course I reacted that way,* she thought to herself. *No one wants to hear that they're letting their family down.*

Because that was exactly what it felt like sometimes when she slept alone in the room that Herman was nice enough to let her borrow. As if she were turning her back on a part of herself, her own flesh and blood. Sure, she tried to help her mother and her younger siblings as much as she could, but the truth? The truth was that she was usually out with Tin-Can and her friends, or busy with some totally unnecessary project that she had come up with to pass the time. The truth was that she would rather tinker around with some of Herman's rusty old cars than call her mother who needed her support. Of course it hurt to realize that.

And now? If she couldn't lean on Tin-Can anymore? What happened then?

"Okay," she said to the ocean. "We'll say that Mr. Sands took something from the horses with his curse. Some sort of energy, maybe. That was possible." Yes, when she thought back to that soot-black, viscous cobweb, she was certain that was the case. And if something was taken, it could also be recovered. They could wake the magic up again. She was sure of it.

The wind was picking up rapidly offshore. It brought tears to her eyes now. There was a rumble, either from the ocean or maybe from the sky. The leaves that were scattered on the ground rustled as they danced a desolate dance. *It almost feels like a storm might be coming,* Alex thought, walking over to a large oak to seek a little shelter. Standing under the tree, she pulled out her phone and texted her friends. *Should we meet at the stables after school tomorrow? We have to get the horses going somehow. Too bad we don't have magical powers or anything . . .*

She added a winking smiley, followed by a bolt of lightning, a star, a moon, and a sun. After mulling it over for a while she added a galloping horse as well. Then she looked out at the dark, foamy ocean, and smiled as she felt her phone vibrate.

# 22

Sometimes it felt like time deliberately crept along at a snail's pace, just to be annoying. That was exactly how it felt the next afternoon when all four Soul Riders were seated on the bus on their way to Jorvik Stables. Usually they walked, but Alex had convinced them that it was a better idea to take public transportation. They sat together in the very back of the bus and sighed audibly every time the bus braked, slowed down slightly, or stopped to pick up new passengers. Outside, the rain beat down on the windowpanes so hard that it felt like it might break them.

Lisa looked out and saw a mother with a baby stroller struggling through the wind and pouring rain. She was carrying a big umbrella that she was struggling to hold on to in the furious wind. The umbrella flipped inside out and started to blow away. The woman ran after it, managing to catch it at the last minute, and tried to flip it back the right way without letting go of her baby stroller. Just as the bus pulled to a stop in front of her, her umbrella blew away, landing across the street in a massive puddle. The woman was left standing there with her baby stroller, shaking her head dejectedly.

"I told you taking the bus was a good idea," Alex remarked dryly.

The speakers crackled and then they heard the bus driver's voice. Normally they liked him. He drove this route every day and always had time for a joke and a kind word. Today his cheerful voice was grating, like fingernails on a blackboard. And when they heard what he had to say, they put their hands to their foreheads and groaned.

"Perhaps you're wondering why we're not following our usual route today? Well, listen up! Unfortunately, we need to take a little detour past the hospital because . . . yes, well, you can see all the water in the roadway over there, my friends. This will put us a bit behind schedule as the new route will take slightly longer than usual. I want to make sure you get there, safe and sound. But don't worry, we'll get there. Eventually. And don't forget, the destination makes the journey worth it!"

"Oh, come on," Alex whined, impatiently drumming on the dirty windowpane.

"I mean, seriously. What are the odds that this would happen today of all days?" Anne exclaimed. "This whole day has been like walking through quicksand, *pink* Pandorian quicksand. I thought four o'clock would never come. I'm so ready for teleportation to be a thing," she added. Linda flashed her a warning look. "I know, I know," Anne continued. "We have to conserve the magic and only use it when absolutely necessary. The last time I teleported us, the big dam nearly broke, so believe me, I am *so* not going to frivolously teleport us to the stables just because the bus is taking a little longer than usual."

"Good," Linda said quickly. "And you're going to have to tell us more about that Pandorian quicksand sometime. But for right now, since we're stuck here, why don't we start coming up with a plan now before we get to the stables?"

Everyone's eyes turned to Lisa, who was scraping some gum off of the sole of her cowboy boot. Linda had noticed that her friend often started fiddling with things when she felt insecure.

Lisa looked up, tossing the scraped-off gum into the small trash can under the window.

"We need to have all the horses together," Lisa said. "I vote we do it in the pasture."

"In this weather?!" Linda blurted out.

"Sorry," Lisa said with a shrug of her shoulders. "But I think it will be easiest that way. Besides, there's a shed with a roof that they can stand under if it continues raining."

Linda looked sadly down at her already mud-splattered tights and her almost completely new high-tops. She had so many strengths, she knew that, but maybe, just maybe, dressing appropriately for the weather wasn't one of them.

"Are you sure that's the best way?" Anne wondered. "Because Concorde starts to run away from me the minute I approach him in the field these days. And that's if I'm lucky." She tried to make it sound like a joke, but her blue eyes filled with tears.

"Oh, Anne, I know how that feels," Linda sighed, hugging her around the shoulders.

Anne rolled up the sleeve of her jacket. Her friends gasped at the clearly visible set of angry plum-red horse bite marks on her bruised skin.

"I don't know what got into him," Anne said, her lips quivering. "I don't know him anymore. We used to cuddle with each other for hours."

"Same thing with Tin-Can. He's not himself," Alex said. "He just sleeps and sleeps."

"Meteor has basically stopped eating," Linda said.

"WHAT?!" Alex and Lisa blurted out in unison. "No way!"

"I didn't believe it either when Linda told me yesterday," Anne said.

"That's *really* bad," Alex said.

"Yup," Linda agreed.

"And Starshine won't gallop with me anymore," Lisa said sadly. "And I know this sounds weird, but his mane and his tail are less blue."

"Before Mr. Sands disappeared through that portal, he put some kind of terrible magical spell on the horses," she said. "That awful black smoke, you know. It came from inside the portal, as if there was something or *someone* in there controlling it."

"Garnok," Linda said, a cold shiver running down her spine.

"Yes," Alex said quietly, looking at Linda for a long time. "I think so, too."

Anne and Lisa shuddered.

"That smoke really zapped Tin-Can," Alex continued. "I'm positive that's why all this is happening. It's as if Mr. Sands took whatever it is that forms our special, unique bond with our horses and messed it up, contaminated it."

Lisa remembered the pale, spider-like hands turning in front of the horses' panic-stricken faces and the hair on the back of her neck stood up.

"The evil magic has affected all four of the horses," Lisa said. "And our bond to the horses was somehow severed. So, I think we all need to be together, the four of us and our horses. I'll do everything I can to try to repair the bond, but I don't know if it'll work."

"Of course it will!" Alex proclaimed. "You healed Starshine's leg, you made one of my giant bruises go away that time, and you healed Linda! You can do this!"

The others nodded enthusiastically, and Lisa felt a warmth spreading through her chest.

*They believe in me*, she thought. *They believe in me even now, when I don't dare believe in myself. That's true friendship.*

That unfamiliar but lovely feeling lasted just until they got off the bus. Lisa even smiled cheerfully at the hopelessly positive bus driver before the doors closed again.

Then they stood there in front of the gilded metal horses that adorned the gates leading to the stable. They had stood there together so many times before, but today it felt different. Fateful. It appeared to have finally stopped raining, but a chilly wind blew in over the stable yard and seized the gate with a desolate jangling sound. For a brief instant it looked as if the gilded horses were dancing in the wind. Then the girls opened the gates and walked in. A jet-black autumn leaf floated down onto Lisa's boot. She picked it up and looked at it.

The last time they had been here, the leaves were bright red. Now they were black and withered, like burnt paper.

"Weird," Alex said. Lisa agreed. Sure, she had seen black leaves before, but as many as this, all at once?

*There's something wrong with Jorvik.* For the first time she allowed herself to think that thought all the way through. *I don't think this is over. Not even close, actually.*

When she dropped the leaf, she noticed that Linda was looking at her with a thoughtful expression.

"All right," Lisa said, taking a deep breath. "Here we go."

## 23

Tin-Can was snoozing in the back of the wind shelter when they arrived at the pasture. His unruly forelock practically covered his eyes, but as they approached, they could see that his closed eyelids were twitching. When Alex reached out her hand to caress his muzzle, he released a long, contented sigh, but his eyes remained shut.

"Hey, sleepyhead," Alex said softly. "Where are your buddies?"

"I see Meteor over there," Lisa said, pointing to the big birch tree some distance away. Sure enough, Meteor was standing there under the tree. His eyes were also closed, and he was swaying back and forth as if he were being rocked by an invisible hand. He didn't open his eyes when they approached. Linda thought he looked like he had lost weight; his normally round belly looked smaller.

"Hey, buddy," Linda said, wrapping her arms around her horse. "We're going to help you become your old self again."

Meteor sighed sleepily in response.

Starshine and Concorde were standing together on the far end of the pasture. Their coats made it obvious that they had very recently taken a mud bath in one of the many mud puddles.

"That's going to be fun to get off later," Lisa said, nodding to her formerly white but now dirty-gray horse. Anne's old favorite, Jupiter, a big and slightly chubby gray horse, stood right beside them.

He looked like he had also participated in the mud bathing: his tail, which was usually bright white, was a soggy grayish brown, and there was also mud splashed up onto his plump belly.

"Mhmm," Anne responded with a wry smile. "Hashtag #dapplegraylove ..."

For as long as anyone could remember, Jupiter had been the riding school's Old Faithful, equally popular with beginners and more experienced riders. He was rarely used for lessons anymore and now mostly provided company for the other horses in the pasture.

Something made Anne walk over to Jupiter first. Despite the mud, his white coat gleamed in the muted afternoon sunlight. He eyed her with curiosity, his ears pricked, as he munched on a blade of grass. She felt a silent, nagging worry in the pit of her stomach as she thought about how Concorde had snapped at her the previous day. So many things were coming to the surface now, things she had forgotten about. Suddenly, she remembered how scared she had been as a brand-new riding student, with her hair in pigtails, wearing her gleaming white, brand-new riding pants (of course they were thoroughly dirty before she had even managed to mount the horse). She had struggled that first day to (unsuccessfully) fend off a grumpy little pony's furtive, angry nips. Her heart had constantly been in her throat, and her arms and thighs were quickly covered with bruises. She didn't dare show anyone how scared she was. But the next time she had a lesson, Herman had made sure she had Jupiter. She had learned to feel safe with him.

She scratched his forehead and thought about how he had carried her all the way to the Secret Stone Circle when she had been forced to go there to save Concorde. Yes, Old Faithful was really an apt description for Jupiter. Plus, he held the highest rank of all the horses in the stable, which meant that the others obeyed him.

Even the Starbreeds, the ones who were a *little extra everything* and were not like any of the other horse breeds, listened to Jupiter. Anne planned to take advantage of that now. She kissed him on the nose and whispered, "Come here, Jupiter. We're going to bring Concorde and Starshine over to the others."

The gray horse with the kind eyes nickered so quietly that only Anne could hear it, and then he started walking toward the wind shelter where the other girls stood with their horses. Concorde and Starshine followed him.

Lisa had already started singing by the time Anne arrived, walking along with the last two horses. Her crystal-clear voice rose into the fall air. Everyone else stood quietly and listened, waiting, breathing. They could almost hear each other's heartbeats, it was so quiet.

Lisa carefully placed her hand on Starshine's withers as she continued to sing. A soft, pink glow spread around her and the horse. Then she did the same with Meteor, and then Tin-Can and Concorde. She did exactly as she had done before when she was healing an injury. She let the melody and the swirls of pink and blue sparks be her guide, leading her into the magic. She sang and clapped, clapped and sang. *Soon,* she thought. Soon they would be back to their usual selves again.

But there was something preventing the magic from reaching the horses. It felt like there was almost a physical barrier. A massive blob blocking the energy. The strong wind found its way into the shelter, carrying the little sparks of magic away with it. A faint pink light ignited, flickered, and then was blown out. Everything became silent and black again. Empty.

"It's not working," she finally said. "Something is blocking me. I can't get through to the horses. Ugh!" She kicked an overturned water bucket, sending it bouncing away. Then in frustration she pulled her hands through her already disheveled red hair so that it was standing straight up. Her friends were filled with compassion as they looked on.

"Don't worry. We'll figure this out," Alex said intently. "We *have* to figure this out."

The others just nodded.

As they brought the horses back from the pasture, their heads were still drooping. When it was time to feed them, Meteor refused to eat his oats, and Concorde kicked at Anne as she tried to brush him. Starshine and Tin-Can just stared listlessly straight ahead. There was no camaraderie, no love, nothing. Everything was just grayness and misery, like the mud puddles out in the pasture.

"It didn't work," Lisa said with a lump in her throat. "What are we going to do?"

They were standing together inside the tack room. They were going to take the bus home right away. It smelled like leather, saddle soap, and horses. Normal smells—but there was nothing normal about this moment.

"I can't heal them," Lisa continued, her eyes sad. "It didn't work, even though the actual magic seemed like it worked. What are we going to do?"

The four friends looked at each other, lost. They searched each other's eyes, hoping to find an answer there. But there was no answer to be found.

How were they supposed to help their horses when even magic didn't work?

"If only Elizabeth were here," Alex said quietly. "She would have told us not to give up, that the power was within us, or something Elizabeth-like. And we would have believed it because she was the one saying it."

"This is never going to work," Linda said. "Not without Elizabeth or some other help."

No one disagreed with her.

They sat in silence on the bus the entire way back into town. When it was time for Anne to change buses to head home to Jorvik City, she stood up and got off without saying goodbye. Through the window, they saw her raise her hand and wave. The others waved back. Then the bus moved on and they sat together in an oppressive, stifling silence.

"Man, the wind is really blowing," Linda said, looking out at the street. A recycling bin had tipped over and cardboard packaging danced around in the battering winds. "The weather's going to be even worse this week."

"I heard that, too," Alex said. "There's supposed to be a real storm coming in a few days. The worst in several decades according to the meteorologists. Can that really be true?"

"I guess we'll find out," Linda replied. The bus lurched due to the ever-increasing wind. Lisa clung to the seat. The bus swerved along, trying to evade all the rubbish that blew out onto the roadway. They were the only passengers left on the bus. No more peppy announcements from the driver anymore.

"I can feel it," Lisa said in a subdued voice as the driver announced her stop. "How we're slipping away from each other as well. It hasn't happened yet, but it's going to happen if the horses don't return to normal again. You guys can feel that, too, can't you?"

Alex and Linda squirmed in the uncomfortable seats. The engine rumbled as the driver changed gears.

"Things are going south so fast," Lisa said. "Were the horses the only thing that was holding us together? This whole time?" she said, walking toward the exit. "Please tell me that wasn't the case."

Linda opened her mouth to say the words that she knew Lisa so desperately needed to hear just then, that they all needed to hear, but she couldn't get a sound out. Lisa looked at her sadly. Then she straightened her backpack and stepped out onto the sidewalk.

Outside, it was getting dark. Night would be upon them soon.

# 24

As the night fell over Jorvik, something was different. Under the cover of darkness, something had shifted. The sensitive ones— the chosen ones—could sense it, like a dull headache, a vague uneasiness that was hard to put a finger on. It was just a hunch, a tingle down the spine. Maybe they woke up in a cold sweat, with the bedsheets twisted, and yelled something right out into the darkness. Although afterward, they couldn't remember what they yelled, or even what it was that woke them up.

The vast majority don't notice anything at all. Sure, people see the wind pick up. People read the news reports about the storm that's said to be on its way. People make sure that they have enough water on hand and bring their pets inside. People hope for the best. Surely it would all be fine.

Or it wouldn't.

Linda lay back down in bed and smoothed out her blanket, her pulse slowly returning to normal again. Down at the foot of her bed, her cat continued to sleep peacefully.

"It was nothing, Misty," she mumbled sleepily and closed her eyes. "Just a dream."

But something was different. Something was about to happen. She just couldn't say what. Not yet . . .

Outside of the sleeping girl's window, the wind increased. The windowpanes would be rattling soon. A branch broke and struck the roof. The girl slept on.

"The storm," she mumbled. "It's coming."

Her unseeing eyes opened for a brief second. All that could be seen was the rolling whites of her eyes. Then she sank deeper into her dream. She was shivering from the cold as she lay under her covers.

She stood at the edge of the water, by a cold, dead ocean. There were fish, jellyfish, and crabs lying motionless in the sand. And other creatures, as if taken from some of the horror books that she loved to read. Prehistoric animals. Aquatic animals. Animals averse to light that dwelled at the bottom of the ocean. We humans weren't meant to see them, but now the ocean had spat them up.

She pulled her hand over one of the creatures, watching how the scaly tail twitched under her touch. She lifted the creature up, which appeared to be half-frog, half-fish, and let it swim out into the ocean again. The water felt cold and sticky in her soaking-wet shoes. She wanted to move back, in toward the shore, but something was keeping her there. What?

The sky above her was unfathomably dark. Then, the sky was lit up by a blinding flash of white light. She squinted, trying to see where the light was coming from.

*There,* a voice said to her, *in the ocean. There's the answer.*

The ocean waves roared, telling her to keep away. Something was calling her, wanting her for something.

*You'll find out now,* the voice whispered. *Everything you need to know in order to proceed. It's all out here. Become one with everything, Linda. Come.*

She took a step out into the water and saw yet another one of the small creatures. Her legs were rigid, numb. The light grew stronger the farther out she went. It seemed to come from the bottom of the ocean, where it pulsed in time with the roar. Was she the one screaming? Her mouth was wide open in a horrified O, but no sound was coming out of it. All she could hear was the angry roar of the ocean.

It wanted her, the ocean. It wanted everything. Nothing would be left once the ocean had gotten what it wanted.

Not the ocean, she realized with a start: Garnok. When Garnok had gotten what he wanted. He would get it soon.

When Linda woke up in her bed, her lungs felt tight, as if she were lying under water. It took a long time before she was able to breathe normally again. Then sleep reclaimed her, and she continued to dream of the ocean and the darkness. And of a ship that was approaching land . . .

Off the coast of Jorvik, a strange ship traveled through the night, gliding silently and majestically along through the troubled waters. Now and then, a dark red, flickering light could be made out among the shadows. The light came from the enormous platform at the very end of that strange ship sailing along slowly through the water. Sparks flew into the icy night air. Deep down on the ocean floor, a muffled, watery roar could be heard.

Although . . . was it really coming from the ocean? The roar rose, becoming a low bellow, almost human. The sound seemed to come from inside the very same glowing-red portal that still stood in the middle of the platform. Farther out to sea, the waves were higher and stronger. Grabbing at the supports underneath the platform, shaking, pounding, and beating at the steel, chrome, and concrete. But Dark Core's crown jewel slid slowly along, completely unaffected.

Something moved inside the machine that held the portal open, beyond the sparks. A gnarled hand groped its way up, scratching, wanting to get out. The light from the portal changed, turning bright white, blinding.

For a moment, only the outstretched hand could be seen. Then a long, skinny arm. And then another arm. A shoulder that was dislocated and hung limply. The movements were jerky, limp, double-jointed. John Sands crawled back out of his own creation, as defenseless as a fly with its wings ripped off. His face was ghastly white in the dark night and covered in red sores. Moaning, he crawled and elbowed his way out onto the platform, landing with a thump and an almost inaudible whimper. There he lay, staring out at the black water. The wind had picked up and was rocking him back and forth on the ground like a helpless child. What was left of his hair flapped in the strong gusts.

His eyes felt like they were burning. His eyelids were singed, covered in blisters, no eyelashes. He blinked several times, taking in the wild, profoundly black waves. He was waiting for him down there. It was almost time.

"Garnok," Mr. Sands moaned. "I saw your eye. You are so close now. Rosalinda . . . ? Are you here, too, my darling? Have you come back to me?"

He groped blindly toward a female figure who towered over his helpless body. All he could see was long, curly hair.

"My Rosalinda had curly hair," he whispered, opening his singed eyes. "Oh, did Garnok send you, my beloved? You have no idea how much I've missed you! There's so much I want to tell you . . ."

"You're right about one thing," the woman answered. "Garnok sent me. But I'm not Rosalinda. I'm Sabine."

"Saaa . . . Sabine?" He flinched and then tried to sit up but failed. Sabine made a face as he reached up with his badly burned hand, reaching for her own, but finally she took it. He squeezed her hand. She made another face.

"Yes, boss," she replied. "I'm here. Welcome back. We have a lot to deal with right now. What are we doing with the horses? We can ride to Jorvik Stables as soon as tonight if you want."

"We don't need the horses." Mr. Sands's voice was a hoarse whisper against the cold concrete. "They're no longer useful. They've been stripped of their magic. All we need is Garnok. He says that he's ready now . . . ready for liberation."

"Music to my ears," Sabine said. With a disgusted look on her face, she detached herself from Mr. Sands's hand and quickly strode away from the platform. Below, deep underwater, a rumbling could be heard.

The storm picked up, whipping the waves. Water splashed against the sides of the massive ship, raining down on the platform, onto Mr. Sands's wound-covered cheeks. He sighed and turned his head, allowing the cold and the wet to refresh everything in him that was burning.

He lay there until the sun started to rise on the horizon. Then, he lifted his aching head and called for help. From inside the enormous ship, heavy footsteps could be heard approaching him.

The pain in his cheeks was almost unbearable. And yet, he couldn't help but smile.

The time would come soon, soon. Jorvik and the world would be changed forever . . .

# 25

The next afternoon, the girls sat perched on the haybales and rustic wooden benches in the old feed room. The wind outside was so strong that the poorly insulated walls creaked. The storm whined and howled like a crying child. Anne looked up from her notes and shook her head.

"That is a crazy amount of wind," she said, peering out of the tiny window. She saw one of the guys who worked at the stable wrestling outside with a haybale that seemed to want to fly away in the gusty winds sweeping through the stable yard. She shook her head again and sat back down. "Still, I'm glad that we're in here and not out there," she said. Linda mumbled her agreement without looking up from her book.

"Why don't we hang out in here more often?" Alex wondered, looking around. "It's so cozy in here!"

The feed room actually *was* cozy. They all agreed. It was located in the very oldest section of the stable and had beautiful mullioned windows and exposed ceiling beams that had been painted black.

Leaky, somewhat-dilapidated boards stuck up out of the floor here and there. Herman was always talking about how they ought to renovate in there, to keep rats and other things away. But that hadn't happened yet. Instead, for years, all of the feed had been stored up in the big loft, which is significantly newer. Even so, the smell lingered in the walls in here. Every now and then you would get a faint whiff of oats or sweet molasses. And hay, of course.

"No one comes in here anymore," Linda said contentedly and pulled some cinnamon buns out of her backpack. "We can talk in peace in here."

"I really hope things go better today," Lisa said, helping herself to a cinnamon bun and then taking a big bite out of it. "With the horses, I mean."

"Well, try to look on the bright side," Alex replied. "At least things can't really get much worse."

"Now that's the spirit!" Linda said, with a grudging smile. Because in spite of everything, it was kind of nice to be able to joke about how tough things were right now. What else could they do?

They were supposed to finish their homework before they rode the horses in the big riding arena. If the horses would let themselves be ridden, that is. That still felt like a very big *if*. Lisa felt like her whole soul was turning gray and gloopy when she thought about the way Starshine looked at her these days. Or maybe more accurately, the way he *didn't* look at her. She sounded meditative when she turned to Anne and said, "You know, I've never been dumped before, never really been in a relationship actually. Horses before guys, you know."

"Yeah, I know," Anne said with a laugh.

"I'm not doing the guy thing yet," Alex interjected and continued mending a worn stirrup strap. "Tin-Can is the only guy in my life and I'm really happy that way."

Lisa blinked at Alex before she said any more.

"So, I don't know what it feels like, being dumped, I mean," Lisa said, folding a piece of straw into a neat little grid as she spoke. "But I can totally imagine that it feels just like this, sort of like being thrown away, like an old bag of junk, you know? I don't even understand what I did?!"

"You didn't do anything!" Anne exclaimed. "This isn't your fault. And it's not Starshine's either."

"I know," Lisa said, sounding unhappy. "Somehow that makes it even worse. Oh, talking about this just makes me feel depressed." She opened her math book again and went back to her equations. *Today of all days, it feels really great to just do some math,* she thought. *You just make sure your calculations are correct and there's your answer, neat and simple.*

But real life wasn't like algebra. There was only chaos. Although in spite of the chaos, homework was front and center now, and the disused feed room was the perfect place when you wanted to let your thoughts flow freely. They could write, chat, and think completely undisturbed.

Out on the farm, the dilapidated old tractor's big engine could be heard spluttering and hissing as Herman drove around. In the feed room, the only sound was the scratching of pencils as they darted across paper. Otherwise, it was quiet, calm, although definitely not peaceful. Lisa had pulled her hood over her ears and was humming to distract herself. Anne's nails were bitten down, most of the glittery blue nail polish scraped off. Alex had dark circles under her eyes. Every now and then she would get up and leave for a bit. She looked paler every time she came back in. Even Linda, who was usually always cheered up by schoolwork, looked a little droopy. Her eyes were bloodshot behind her round glasses.

"I had a terrible dream last night," Linda said, setting down her book. "In my dream, Mr. Sands came back. He crawled out of that awful portal and basically . . . worshipped Garnok. It makes me feel sick just thinking about it."

Alex shuddered. She had let the stirrup strap drop onto the floor.

"Linda," Lisa said tentatively, putting her hand over Linda's. "That wasn't a dream, right? That was . . . something else."

"A vision," Anne added. "Ugh, tell me it isn't true."

Linda didn't respond immediately, just absentmindedly rubbed her hand over something that had been carved into the bench she was sitting on, maybe by some former riding school student. A heart with two initials, clumsily carved into the wood. It felt rough under her palm. Moisture, dust, and the passage of time had made it impossible to read what it said. Linda kept running her hand over the rough little heart. She wondered if it was a horse or a person and if that even mattered.

"I think it was a vision," Linda said. "Yes. Or a warning. Mr. Sands isn't just going to give up. We should probably have realized that right away."

"So, I mean, it's all well and good that evil wizards can return," Alex said and spat out her gum. "But we actually have other more pressing issues to worry about right now. Like our horses for example! If they even *are* our horses anymore. Tin-Can is like a totally different horse. I don't understand it. And I have no idea how to help him. So, I don't know . . ."

"Alex," Linda said cautiously. "Shh." She looked around; her eyes focused on something behind Alex's back. They sensed a faint humming in the air, an electrical charge. The weird black leaves outside of the window started swirling around in the wind that had suddenly picked up even more.

They heard Herman yell.

Everyone except for Alex rushed over to the little window and looked out. The saw a figure hurry inside through the stable doors.

The figure had its back turned to them and was wearing a big, gray cloak so they couldn't see who it was, not for sure.

But they recognized the cloak. Boy, did they!

There was a tingle in Alex's hand. She jumped at the sudden heat. The others were talking over each other in cutoff sentences.

"Could that . . . ?"

"Is that . . . ?"

"Nooo . . . !"

Then the door opened and someone stepped in.

Linda gasped for breath. Her legs felt weak, and suddenly she flopped right down onto the haybales on the floor. Her friends saw her faint, but they couldn't move to help her.

## 26

It was as if they were all frozen. Linda's mouth hung wide open and her eyes shone. She was still trembling as she slowly got up from the floor. Lisa just had a goofy grin, and Anne looked as if she might faint. They were all staring at something behind Alex. Alex slowly turned around. Her heart sped up faster, faster, faster.

Then time stopped, and Alex's lips broke into the biggest smile ever. A brightly colored butterfly of happiness fluttered to life in her heart. She stumbled to her feet. Her legs trembled, not really wanting to stand. She had to rub her eyes. Could it be true? Could it really be true?

Before her stood a woman dressed in gray with radiant red hair and a friendly face. Alex would recognize that face anywhere. She had only recently become convinced that she would never see it again.

"Elizabeth!" she whispered, her hands flying up to her face. Her cheeks were wet with tears. "Is it really you? Not just some kind of sick illusion? Please tell us you're real, because I don't think I could cope otherwise."

"It's me, I promise," Elizabeth said with a laugh, reaching her arms out into the air. "You have no idea how nice it is not to be a will-o'-the-wisp!"

"I think we have some idea," Linda said. And then they all threw themselves at Elizabeth in one overjoyed group hug. Elizabeth laughed as she tumbled to the ground. She fell down into the warm embrace of straw and flapping arms. And the others fell with her, including Linda, who had only just managed to get back up onto her feet.

Falling had never felt so wonderful.

"It wasn't exactly easy to transform back, obviously," Elizabeth said after they had finished hugging even more, crying tears of joy, and cheering so that it echoed throughout the stable. Everyone talked over each other. The air bubbled with questions.

When? Who? Where?

*How?*

Yes, how? Elizabeth continued recounting. Four pairs of eyes watched her attentively, basking in her twinkling eyes, her calm, happy charisma. It really *was* her!

"The last thing I remember is Pi, out there on the bridge," she said, suddenly looking serious. "A flash of light, and then her hand. It was so gnarled as it reached for me, like a sharp branch. I was scared. I remember that I ran away from Pi and the bridge. Then everything just went dark. I felt myself flicker and disappear. I was sure that I had died."

Linda shivered despite the warmth among them. She blinked quickly to get rid of the terrible images that filled her head. The druid Pi's awful arms and legs, like hard, twisted wood. Elizabeth's horse Calliope, who disappeared into the dark, gurgling swamp water. They couldn't save her. And then Pi's triumphant, hoarse cackle as Elizabeth dissolved into an intense, sparkling bit of light.

"After that, I don't remember anything until the moment I woke up on the ground at the Secret Stone Circle this morning," Elizabeth continued. "The Baroness was there, and Fripp and the druids. Of course, I called out your names. For a brief moment, it felt like I was still there, back with Pi. Then they told me everything I had missed while I was . . . while I was away. Wow, you guys have been busy! I'm so proud of you, girls! You did it. All on your own!"

"To be totally honest, I don't think the druids are very happy with us," Alex said, making a face. "We kind of neglected to tell them that we were going off to try and save Lisa's father. And we ditched Avalon in the woods, too."

"Do you know what?" Elizabeth asked, shaking her head. "As Soul Riders, sometimes you have to make decisions quickly. You have to do what's right. And I happen to know that the druids aren't annoyed or unhappy with you. True, that really was a huge risk that you guys *and* Lisa's father took. You have to understand that."

"But . . . ?" Lisa asked meaningfully.

"But I understand why you did it," Elizabeth said. "And you did the right thing. The druids and Fripp were proud, too. I know that. They're just not that good at expressing it."

The girls laughed.

"Yeah, well that's certainly *one* way to look at it," Linda said. "Oh, Elizabeth, have I said how happy I am to see you?"

"Not for a whole minute," Elizabeth laughed. "I'm happy to see you, too, just so you know. We have so much to talk about. Not least of all what happened to your horses."

"Our horses? But how . . . ?" the girls began, all taking over each other.

"Herman told me how they've been acting," Elizabeth said. "As soon as the druids said that I was fine, I came here to the stable to see you girls. It's hard to be here around the horses so soon after losing Calliope. Beautiful, beautiful Calliope." Her gray eyes grew dark with grief. "I miss her so much. I'm sure I'll hear her screaming in my sleep tonight and for many nights to come, but I heard that you needed my help."

She took a deep breath. "Herman has been so understanding. He even promised that he would arrange a new horse for me, and soon."

"Sooner than you think, my dear Elizabeth," a familiar voice called out. They turned around and gasped when they saw Herman walking toward them down the stable aisle. He was leading a dapple-gray horse in a halter.

"This here is Calenthe," he said and beamed as he saw all their reactions.

A sigh of admiration spread among the girls. Then they ran to Herman and the horse. The sadness in Elizabeth's eyes faded, just slightly.

"She's so much like Calliope," Linda exhaled, cautiously stroking the mare's silky, well-currycombed neck. The others crowded into the aisle so they could pet her, too. She was small and dainty like an Arabian, but still made a surprisingly big and powerful impression. She looked like a fairy tale horse, as if she had stepped right out of a dream.

She was perfect.

"Hi, Calenthe," Anne whispered. She kissed the horse's velvety soft muzzle. She felt a pang when she realized how much she longed to be able to do this very same thing with Concorde again. She was closer to this horse standing in front of her, which she had never seen before, than her own horse right now. That was a painful realization, but Calenthe's gentle breaths against her cheek helped console her a little.

"Where did you find her, Herman?" Alex wondered. They had known since they had found out that they were Soul Riders that Herman was a sort of a horse scout for the druids. He helped select suitable horses for the Soul Riders and the druids. On the other hand, none of them were really clear on how it all really worked. But there was no denying that Herman was indeed very good at his job. Calenthe was radiant, gray, and wise, just like Elizabeth. And like Calliope had been.

"She's from Valedale originally," Herman replied. "In the fields where Calliope galloped as a little foal. I'm guessing they're somehow related, or . . . how do you describe that exactly?"

Elizabeth simply nodded. Her eyes returned to a sparkling light gray again. The darkness had dissipated in the moment, but everyone knew she carried Calliope deep in her heart. Today and every other day. You never forget a beloved horse. You keep on going, one day at a time. You let new horses into your heart, but the other horses remain in there as well. Always.

Herman finally wandered off. The girls kept petting Calenthe, who seemed to enjoy the attention. Elizabeth just stood back, watching the scene unfold before her. She looked pleased but a bit sad at the same time. Lisa got goosebumps as she thought about and realized how close she had been to losing her own horse, too. If Mr. Sands hadn't been kicked into the portal, who knows what could have happened?

In all the commotion over Calenthe, they had completely forgotten what they had been discussing before Elizabeth arrived. It took a while before Anne finally brought the topic up again.

"You mentioned our horses before," Anne said to Elizabeth. "Do you have any idea what happened to them or what we can possibly do to get them back to the way they were? Because we've tried magic and medicine, and nothing seems to help. This just feels so hopeless. I think Concorde hates me."

"He does not," Linda said. "It's not *him*, Anne. It's the spell or hex or whatever has taken over him. But Concorde loves you. You mustn't believe anything else!"

"Linda's right," Elizabeth said with a nod. "Believe me when I say that you have what it takes to save the horses. You don't need my help. You carry the power, the will, and the love inside yourselves. You just have to give the horses time to heal. The horses have absorbed the dark magic, but their bond with you has not been broken as you may have felt. A bond that strong isn't so easily broken, but it's now worn and frayed and in need of mending. I hope you can understand what I mean."

They nodded slowly and Elizabeth continued, "Believe in yourselves and each other. Get out into the countryside with the horses, into the wilderness. Ride together in the woods, in nature. Heal and rest, because you all need that just as much as the horses, every one of you. When the time comes, you'll be ready. As long as you stick together, everything will work out."

Elizabeth smiled warmly at the girls. Lisa was smiling, too, when she felt Alex nudge her in the side.

"I'm going to ride back to the Secret Stone Circle now. Here," Elizabeth added and gave Alex an envelope with ornate handwriting on it. "I wrote down a little more about what you need to do here. Read it in peace and quiet before you set out. There are many of us who will be waiting for you when you're ready."

Alex stuffed the envelope into her jacket pocket and nodded.

"But how are we going to know when we're ready?" Anne protested.

"You'll know," Elizabeth replied as she bridled Calenthe, just as Linda ran off to grab a saddle for her. "One last thing," she said when she was done. Her smile had disappeared now. "It's not over yet. You do understand that, right? A storm is on its way here, and this is no ordinary storm. There's nothing natural about this storm. I think you suspect what—or maybe *who*—is behind it."

"Garnok?" Alex said in a gravelly voice. "Garnok's behind this, right?"

Elizabeth nodded slowly.

"It is your destiny that matters now—Jorvik's destiny," Elizabeth said.

Something burned inside Lisa's head. A sharp swish, like electricity, spreading through her entire body, from her head down to her toes. *No,* she thought, *this is no ordinary storm.*

An icy gust blew open the door to the stable. Anne shivered in her quilted jacket. Lisa took Linda's limp, cold hand and gave it a squeeze.

"I'll see you soon. Maybe sooner than you expect," Elizabeth said and started leading Calenthe outside.

They stood and watched them walk away, observing in silence through the open stable door as Elizabeth mounted and rode away. Then, when the beautiful horse and rider could only be faintly made out as a gray shadow in the distance, the silence was broken.

"You heard what she said," Linda said. "We need to get our horses back now, no matter what it takes."

"What if we can't do it?" Anne glanced over at Concorde who stood dozing in his stall. "What if Garnok has grown too strong?"

"We're stronger," Alex replied firmly. "We can do this, together . . . maybe."

"Maybe?" Lisa repeated.

"That's the strongest statement I felt like I could possibly make right now," Alex said with a shrug. "Come on, we've got a lot to do."

Lisa walked over to Starshine's stall and stood there for a moment before opening the stall door. Normally, he would hear her coming and say hello to her with a muffled nicker, a very slight neigh. Now he didn't even bother lifting his head. This hurt her heart tremendously.

"Maybe might not be enough," Lisa yelled to Tin-Can's stall, where Alex was. "We *have* to help our horses get back to normal. Because otherwise"—she interrupted herself, running her hand over Starshine's neck— "otherwise I don't know what I'm going to do."

The stable's windowpanes were rattling desolately in the wind. Inside the stall, Alex wiped a tear from her cheek. She didn't know if this was an angry tear or a sad tear. Did it even really matter? Normally, Alex would put a stop to her tears as soon as she felt them burning inside her.

She liked being angry better than being sad, because she could accomplish things with anger; she could take action. She let her tears fall now, one after another. Was it just her imagination or did Tin-Can twitch when they landed on his shaggy neck? Did he look perkier all of a sudden, or was it just her, hoping so fervently it would be true?

"Oh, forget *maybe*," she said to the wall. She could tell from Lisa's breathing, on the other side, that she was also fighting tears. As much as she wished Tin-Can would return to his normal, perky self, Alex wished that Lisa wouldn't have anything to cry about. But things were the way they were for now. As they stood in their own stalls, hearing each other cry, it felt a little bit comforting somehow to know that they were not alone. Alex rested her forehead against Tin-Can's and then she said to Lisa, but also to herself, "Let's do this."

## 27

A scrawny farmer in overalls and a flat cap peered at the four young riders and their horses as they approached him in the cloudy morning light.

"Are you really going out riding in this weather, girls? This is the worst storm I've ever seen in my whole life, and you should know that I've seen some storms in my day. It was sheer luck that I managed to get all of the animals outside in time after the place was struck by lightning last night."

He was standing beside what was left of a large barn that had been completely burned to the ground. He shook his head sadly. Wood and debris were scattered all around him: stacks of hay and animal feed, tools, a large pitchfork.

There was a pungent, thick smell. It smelled burnt. Tin-Can sniffed the air and flattened his ears back. Alex wondered if he could sense the fear of the animals that had been inside the barn when it caught fire.

"We won't be out for long. We promise. We're going to school afterward," Alex said, stroking Tin-Can's neck. "It's a relief to hear that all of your animals are okay."

Two days had passed since they had met Elizabeth in the stable. The storm had only grown worse since then—but something else had improved. They could feel a difference now. Their horses didn't just accept being ridden, but actually welcomed it. Everything wasn't back to normal yet. *Maybe it would never be normal again,* Lisa thought as she rode along in the back on Starshine. But they had seemed to have found some sort of new normal. It seemed as if, together, they would be able to restore the horses and themselves.

Lisa gave the old man a friendly smile and a wave.

"Do you have anywhere for your animals to stay until you can rebuild your barn?" she wondered and glanced over her shoulder toward the pine trees, which were shaking in the strong winds.

"Oh yes," the man replied. "Not to worry. Plenty of people have offered to help. Things always work out . . ."

They trotted away from the old farmer's destroyed barn, straight into the woods. The old man stood watching them until the sound of their horses' hooves disappeared and all that could be heard was the wailing of the wind. Then he returned to picking pieces of the wreckage up off of the ground.

The trail wound around, twisting here and there now that they were heading deeper into the woods. It was a windswept morning late in October and the Soul Riders were out riding again. Yes, they finally felt like Soul Riders again, all four of them. It had been a while since they had felt that way.

"Have you ever thought about how sometimes we ride together as Soul Riders and sometimes as ourselves—I mean our regular selves?" Anne asked. "It feels a bit like riding with or without armor on, doesn't it?"

Alex looked at her for a long time before responding.

"And yet we're always Soul Riders," Alex said. "That's the thing, isn't it? Even when we don't feel like Soul Riders, we are. Maybe then most of all."

"You're probably right," Anne said, a little surprised. "I just hadn't thought of it that way."

The majestic firs around them shook in the stormy weather. The sky was such a dark gray that it was nearly black, and the powerful wind caused their eyes to tear up. The horses were moving a little faster now. Tin-Can's ears were pricked forward the way they usually were when he smelled something exciting and wanted to investigate what it was.

The world still felt gray, and the magic far away, but even so they all felt calmer as they rode together farther into the forest, toward the promising pink glow that revealed there was a runestone nearby.

*Nature is your oasis, your safe place. Ride out into it and feel how the horses slowly recover and rejuvenate. Take in the woods and the fresh air. Pay particular attention to runestones. They're all over the place, if you know where to look. The glow of the runes along with being out in nature and being with you will make the horses feel better.*

That was what Elizabeth had written in the letter that they had read together several times. Although right now the woods didn't exactly feel like a safe place to be, Lisa thought, listening to the sound of a branch snapping in the strong wind. But it seemed like Elizabeth was right. Something did feel easier. Starshine was moving differently now, more like himself. As they approached a runestone, he broke into a canter without her doing anything at all.

*I'm going to keep hoping for a miracle*, she thought as Starshine abruptly slowed down and his head drooped.

Because miracles did happen. They happened all the time. It's just that people often missed them, because no one ever knew where to look.

Linda shivered in the chilly air and thought about what Elizabeth had said. *It's not over yet. You do understand that, right?* To be told that something was going to happen but not to be able to see it yourself was like sitting in the back seat and watching someone else drive full speed toward a cliff, she thought. She felt powerless. Why wasn't she having any visions? She knew they were in there somewhere, but she couldn't access them.

*Because I need Meteor's strength. We need all of our horses, the bond with them. We're nothing without that, just like we're nothing without each other.* That thought resonated with her, and she realized that it was really true. They wouldn't be able to get their powers back until the horses were themselves again.

She impatiently urged Meteor on and glanced up at the runestone, which they could now see clearly up on a moss-covered hill. The island's secrets and wisdom awaited them up there. That was where the magic would reawaken. Maybe it had already begun to do so.

They had met at the stables every day and ridden out into the forest together, just like Elizabeth had instructed them to do. It didn't really feel quite normal, not yet. But surely things were going in the right direction. Yes, they agreed on that, all four of them. This morning as Anne was grooming him, Concorde had leaned against her shoulder. She began to cry when she had felt the warmth of his big, heavy head. It had been such a long time since he had wanted to be close to her. The bruise on her arm had started to fade from an angry bluish-red to a faint yellowish-green. She wasn't scared of him anymore.

Anne never wanted to be scared again. Not of her own horse, not that Mr. Sands would return, not of the wobbly pink unreality in Pandoria. She didn't want to be scared that her mother would mock her when her dressage practice didn't go as she had planned, or that someone at school would call her *princess* and turn up their nose at her as if they had smelled something bad. Enough was enough, she thought, noticing how the rising sun shimmered in Concorde's gray mane. The period of fear was behind them. They were entering into something new now, she and her friends. She didn't know what. She didn't know how, where, or why, either. But she did know that she would be ready when she needed to be. Could the others see that, too? Anne felt like she was holding her head higher. It was like the ride was making her stronger. She had ridden here on her own on Jupiter when she needed to save Concorde from Pandoria. Now she would save him one more time. She would save him again and again, as many times as necessary.

She still didn't know what the rest of the world thought when they saw her, but she knew one thing: it didn't matter anymore.

Up on the hill, Anne saw how the colors of the last of the fall leaves were competing with the light from the runestone. She felt a fire inside her, too. She turned to Lisa, who was riding behind her, and smiled broadly. Lisa returned her smile but was startled when she suddenly heard Alex yell out. Tin-Can had stumbled on the barren, rocky path leading up to the runestone. Linda, who was riding in the back, gasped as she saw how close Alex came to falling off and landing on the sharp rocks below.

Alex tried to collect herself. "Normally he's as surefooted as a mountain goat," she said in a shaky voice. "I keep forgetting that he's not himself."

Alex's pulse was still throbbing out of control. Every now and then she glanced back over her shoulder. She couldn't help thinking about how close she'd come to falling off. No doubt she would have escaped with some serious scrapes, at the very least. She suddenly felt powerless and—well—scared.

"Sorry, pal," she whispered into Tin-Can's shaggy ear. "I'm so used to you helping me through everything. I'm the one who has to help you now." Tin-Can let out a long sigh. Was she imagining things, or did he sound slightly relieved? They moved on, more slowly now. The runestones above them glowed pink and silver.

Alex looked up and felt that her legs had stopped shaking. She could breathe once again. One by one they stopped in front of the runestone. Their hands felt warm against their horses. A soft pink glow spread from the runestone and rained down upon them. A tense, jittery expectation hung wordlessly in the air. *It's time.* Then Lisa sang for them. *The time is now.* Never before had the words felt so true. The song floated out of her, toward the runestone and the horses.

It was nice to break into song for a change. Singing and song-writing were what mattered most to Lisa, not talking. Sometimes it felt as if she was talking about a completely different person when she tried to talk about herself. Her songwriting came so naturally, so she sang instead. The colors and the sharpness came back to her. She didn't want to be anywhere else in the whole world then. The glow from the runes was reflected in Lisa's eyes and the song wafted up into the dark clouds.

As long as she was singing, time stood still. As long as she was singing, it felt like anything was possible. It wasn't until the last clear note had faded away that they slowly realized the spell was broken. In the meantime, there was practically a hurricane going on around them, with hard, freezing winds. Above the forest and the blue mountain peaks in the distance, there was an ominous rumbling. Below them, on the trail they had just ridden up in the valley, they saw the trees whipping viciously back and forth.

"Uh-oh," Alex said, looking down. "That doesn't look good."

A sharp crack, like a thunderclap, made them jump.

"Did you see that?!" Linda yelled, pointing. "That tree over there just split right in two!"

"We've got to ride back to the stables!" Lisa exclaimed.

Alex nodded grimly and then hopped off of Tin-Can and carefully started leading him down the rocky slope, back onto the trail. She didn't want to risk coming that close to falling off again.

"We can cut through the big field. Then we'll get home faster," Alex said.

They settled into a gentle trot together. Lisa glanced at Linda and saw that they were riding perfectly in step with each other. The horses' legs moved like twins over the ground. She caught Linda's eye, leaned forward in her saddle, and grinned when Starshine switched into a canter, just what she had been hoping for. Linda and Meteor followed their example, then Alex and Tin-Can, and finally Anne and Concorde. They cantered together, faster and faster. For a little while it felt like the storm around them had blown over. Lisa heard a soft, insistent sound and realized to her surprise that she was singing again.

"Wow!" Alex said as they slowed down and looked at each other, their cheeks flushed. "It's been a while since we did that."

Lisa didn't answer, wanting to stay in the moment forever, which would end far too soon. She leaned over Starshine's neck and gave him a big hug.

"Now we ride home, pretty boy," she said and felt the wind pick back up around them once again. Her eyes watered with tears. Starshine pricked up his ears and broke into a gallop.

Crisp, dry grass stuck up in the field in straggly tufts. They could hear the wind moving through the grasses inside the empty fences where some of Jorvik's ponies usually grazed. All around, they saw toppled trees, little ramshackle sheds with tattered roofs. Moldering fall leaves whirled desolately around and around in the biting wind. Linda felt the cold on her cheeks and wondered, dazed from the wind, if the saying was *the calm after the storm* or *the calm before the storm.* She could never remember.

She told Meteor to giddy up and he sped up. His shaggy ears were attentive, his eyes trained on the empty field. Linda patted him tenderly.

"You're wondering what's up with the weather, too, aren't you, Meteor?" she said. "We all are."

But inside she was cheering, despite the wind. He had done exactly what she'd said! She sought out Alex's eyes and thought she could make out the hint of a smile on her friend's face. Suddenly it grew quieter around them. The wind's howling wasn't as obvious anymore.

It was as if her reconnecting with Meteor had weakened the wind around them. Although just a little, little bit. As they rode closer to Jorvik Stables, the wind's strength picked back up, making them hunker down in their saddles.

They could still hear the wind howling in their ears after they slammed the stable door closed and led their tired, dazed horses into their stalls a short while later.

"Finally!" Herman exclaimed as he rushed into the stable, spotting them as they closed their horses' stall doors one by one and then stepped out into the aisle with their saddles and bridles in their arms. Herman's usually very calm blue eyes flitted back and forth anxiously, and he was pulling on the thin, white hair on the top of his head when he continued, "I was starting to get really worried! I just listened to the weather forecast and heard that the storm is expected to reach hurricane strength off the coast overnight. Myself and all of the stable staff have been storm-proofing the stables all morning, lashing down carts and bringing in all the loose items from the courtyard. No one should be out in this weather. Promise me that you won't go out riding again!"

"Oh, we won't," Linda replied. "And anyways, we have to get to school."

"School?" Herman stared at her, wide-eyed. "Haven't you been following the news at all, girls? The schools are all closed until further notice. They announced it earlier this morning."

"It must have happened while we were out riding. Whoops," Linda said and laughed, slightly embarrassed. But inside she felt a sudden chill. This was for real. Alex ran her hand over her jacket pocket. She didn't need to pull out the letter to remind them what it said.

*Ancient energies are in motion. Jorvik's primordial forces are being unleashed—and you need to stop them.*

She let go of her thoughts of Elizabeth and the letter and turned to Herman instead. There was a frightening clattering sound up on the roof.

"I hope those beams are strong," Alex said.

"This place has been standing since the time of Jon Jarl," Herman said with a nod. "It would take a lot more than this storm to bring down Jorvik Stables."

Linda looked around, taking in the sturdy ceiling beams and the stone walls that she had seen so many times before. *Yes,* she thought. *Herman was probably right. But what would it take to bring us down? How much can we withstand?*

As she looked into her friends' eyes, she realized that they were all thinking the same thing.

Lisa sighed and started walking toward Starshine's stall. Her footsteps were heavy, almost procrastinating. She didn't expect anything. So, she didn't respond right away when Starshine stuck his head out and gave her that gentle, nickering greeting she had missed so much.

"Oh, buddy!" She flung her arms around his neck. Starshine nudged her head with his. When she looked into his eyes, they were clear.

"You guys . . . ?" she said tentatively to the others.

Anne pressed her face to Concorde's neck, and he let her do it, too. More than let her, he nudged her in return. He gave her a kiss with his soft muzzle. She felt the warmth from his nostrils and grinned.

"I think it worked," she finally said, her eyes sparkling.

"Yeah," Linda said from inside Meteor's stall, wiping her eyes when she saw how he pounced on the oats that had been sitting untouched in his manger. His brownish-red coat was shiny again, and his long, snow-white mane had its luster back.

"WE'RE BACK! Woohoo!" Alex shouted, popping out into the aisle. She was so jubilant that she forgot about Tin-Can, who came thundering out of his stall door and ran a cheerful victory lap over to Meteor's half-open stall. He moved like a mischievous colt out for a romp. He was Tin-Can again.

Alex let her horse mess around a little. A haybale tumbled down, becoming the perfect snack for him and Meteor. The two horses raced each other down the aisle.

"It looks like they're dancing," Linda said, laughing and watching the two horse friends as they trotted around in the hay. Then she grabbed Alex's hand and did a little happy dance herself.

*It worked.*

"What do we do now?" Lisa asked. She couldn't take her eyes off Starshine; she couldn't get her fill of looking at him.

"Now we get ready," Anne replied. "You remember what Elizabeth said. Tomorrow we ride to the Secret Stone Circle. There's nothing that can stop us now: no school, no un-magical horses."

"Tomorrow?" Lisa said. She would have to talk to her father tonight then. A knot formed in her stomach. How was she going to get him to understand that she *had* to do this? And that they could never move away from Jorvik, because this was her home. This was where her fate would be decided.

Her hand went up to Starshine's nose. She felt his heat, how there were sparks between them again. And then she knew that it didn't matter *how*. She just had to make her father understand. And if he refused to listen, then she would go anyway.

They couldn't wait any longer.

# 28

That same evening, Lisa sat with her father in the living room while they watched TV. He drank coffee and she had tea. The storm whined outside the windows, louder and louder. The rain beat on the roof. The bluish glow from the TV gave her father's face a ghostly pallor that made him look almost transparent. Inside the TV, a man in a red blazer pointed at a weather map, smiling nervously.

"Dad . . . ?" Lisa said hesitantly. "We have to talk."

"I know," he replied. But then he didn't say anything else. His eyes were back on the lit-up screen, where the weatherman continued discussing the storm.

"This may well be the storm of the century," the meteorologist said, suddenly looking serious. "We don't know exactly when it's expected to reach full strength, but we could be talking about hurricane-force winds. So far, the brunt of the storm has remained offshore, but we ask you to keep up to date on the weather front and to stay home. We will be broadcasting beyond our regular hours due to the new storm warning in effect for . . ."

Cut to a story from a supermarket where two women were fighting over a large pack of bottled water.

Cut to the sign by Pinta Bay, engulfed in floodwaters.

Cut to a terrified wild horse being captured out on the plains and transported away.

"Dad?" Lisa said again, more impatiently this time. "I have to leave. Tomorrow morning. Me and the other girls. There's something we need to take care of. It's related to the storm and a bunch of other stuff that I don't have time to explain right now. But, please, you have to let me go riding. And whatever you do, don't follow me. Promise me that!" She paused for a moment. An emergency phone number flashed across the TV screen in big, bright numbers. *Call this number if you require evacuation assistance.*

"We'll already be far away from here, I hope, before it comes down to evacuating the island," her father said and took a big gulp of his coffee.

Lisa set her cup down with a bang.

"You're not listening to me! We *need* to stay here on Jorvik. This is where I belong. If we move, I'm putting my friends in danger. Do you understand?"

Her father reached for the remote control and switched off the TV. The images of Jorvik's wind-whipped coastline and high, gray surf faded to black and then disappeared. Lisa looked at her father, waiting for him to say something. The clock ticked, irritatingly slowly. There was a click as the coffee machine in the kitchen turned itself off.

Finally, in a voice that was quieter and gentler than his usual Dad-voice, he said, "There's so much I'm trying to understand, things that are barely understandable. I'm so worried about you, sweetie—about you and your friends. It's way too dangerous, the stuff you've gotten mixed up in. Please, drop it. Come back to Texas with me! We can get ourselves a small house on the prairie. You can have a horse. Maybe we could even bring Starshine. I can talk to Herman, make him an offer that he can't refuse." He smiled and wiggled his eyebrows a little, the way he always used to do when Lisa was little and he wanted to make her laugh.

But Lisa wasn't laughing this time.

"Dad, I am *not* going to move away from Jorvik! And Starshine can't leave the island. He's a Starbreed. Starbreeds have to stay here. So I'm staying here, too, with Starshine and my friends. I would rather die than move."

He winced as if she had slapped him.

"That's exactly what I'm afraid of, darling. It's far too dangerous here. And now all this business with the storm . . ." He looked out the window, listening to the storm howling and roaring. "I just don't want to lose you, too. You and I know what it feels like to lose someone you love. I never want to go through that again."

"Me either," Lisa said gently, taking a seat closer to her father, close enough that she could feel him trembling. "But, Dad, how were you thinking we would get out of here, anyway? They've shut down all the ferries for the time being. The airport is closed, too. They haven't decided on the safest way of evacuating."

Her father sighed again.

"Yes, on some level I understand that it isn't possible to get out of here *right now*. But I don't see us in Jorvik a few years from now. I thought I did. I had hoped so. But it's simply too dangerous. I just need you to understand, Isa. You're all I have. I worry myself sick when I think about what might happen. Jorvik is a dangerous place. I know that and you know that."

"Believe me, I know," Lisa replied. "You said that already."

"Well, it's worth repeating," her father said. She looked at him and thought that his eyes seemed clearer than before, more decisive. She gave him a quick pat on the hand. Then she looked him straight in the eye and said, "We're going to get through this.

We're going to pull this off. I promise. You and me against the world, right?"

Her father's gold tooth flashed when he smiled. Lisa felt a spark of inspiration, which gave her courage. She reached for her father's hand and gave it a squeeze. She knew how to get her father to listen now.

"I know, Dad," she said, looking him right in the eye. "I *know*. Everything you've been through . . . it's connected to things my friends and I have faced. I have so much I need to tell you, but I don't know if I can or if I'm allowed to. But my friends and I, we have to go. Now, before the storm arrives and takes everything away. There's not much time!"

Carl turned the TV back on. The screen filled once again with galloping horses, their manes flying in the storm winds.

"In many parts of the island, here in Winter Valley for example, local animal lovers are working together to try to capture the grazing wild horses," the reporter said. "But it's a race against time, as the winds are predicted to reach hurricane force soon. Will there be time to save the horses? This is one of the many questions Jorvik residents are all asking themselves right now."

In the news broadcast, a Jorvik Wild Horse broke loose and ran off into the woods. Her father pointed to the TV screen.

"Say what you want about Jorvik, but at least people take care of their horses here."

"Add that to the list of reasons not to move," Lisa mumbled, setting down her mug of tea.

Her father wrung his hands nervously, the way he usually did when he wanted to say something but was having trouble spitting it out. Finally, with his eyes glued to the TV screen, he said, "Remember those horse books you devoured when you were little— your mom's old collection? We could hardly interact with you; you were so absorbed in them. To think that you've found your way back to horses again. In spite of everything that's happened since we moved to Jorvik, I'm grateful for that: that I got to see you happy here, with Starshine and your new friends."

Lisa remembered, too. The hours had flown by, lying on her stomach in bed and binge-reading book after book. The happy heroine always got her horse in the end. Then, after Lisa's mom died in a horseback riding accident, she threw away every last book. Everything she had learned about horses was a lie. There was no happy ending.

Now, suddenly, she missed the feeling she had once gotten from reading those books. Maybe it had been a mistake to get rid of them. She never thought that she would want to have anything to do with horses again, but then she met Starshine. She leaned over her steaming mug of tea to hide the tears in her eyes, blowing cautiously before taking a big sip and swallowing.

"But, Dad?" she said quietly. "I don't want to just talk about horses right now. I want to talk about why I have to stay here in Jorvik. We can't move away. Do you understand that? My friends and I, we have to stay. And it's related to some of the things that happened on the platform after we rescued you. And a bunch of other stuff that I can't get into right now."

Her father sat quietly, holding his empty coffee cup. It felt like several hours went by before he finally looked up.

"I think I understand, and I'm going to help you in every way I can," he said quietly. "It hurts to know that you're in danger, but I suppose I have to let you go. Anything else would be wrong of me, selfish. You have an important job to do. I understand that, even though you haven't told me much."

"Dad," Lisa said. "There's a lot that I need to tell you later, that I *want* to tell you. You know that, right? How we were able to break into Dark Core Headquarters, for example. And what I was actually doing during fall break . . ."

He waved his hand dismissively.

"You don't owe me anything. I, on the other hand, will be eternally indebted to *you*. I don't know how long I would have lasted in that prison cell. Lisa," he said, looking tenderly at his daughter. "I trust that you'll eventually tell me everything. But right now, the most important thing of all is that you and your friends are able to do what you need to do. I'd be lying if I said that I wasn't worried, that I wasn't dying of curiosity about what you're actually up to. But I know that you'll do the right thing. You're growing up, sweetie. You're old enough to make the right decisions on your own. I forget that sometimes."

A wave of warmth swelled in Lisa's chest.

"Thank you," she said and gave her father a kiss on the cheek. Then she leaned her head against his shoulder, just like she used to when she was little. He still used the same aftershave. The smell of it made her feel safe, made her keep forgetting about all of the dark things while the wind howled outside the window.

The sun had set. They could hear a dog barking at the house next door, nearly drowned out by the wind. Lisa's father scratched his scalp and then continued talking.

"You and your friends can make a real difference. I've been sitting here at home at my wits' end, contemplating it from every angle, trying to think of some other way out. I don't want to send my daughter and her best friends out on their own. It hurts me to think that you've already met Mr. Sands. I just want, I don't know, to wrap you up in cotton wool and make you guys hamburgers. But I have to let you go, I get that. And like I said, I promise not to ask any questions. You'll always be my child, but children have the right to have secrets. I trust you with my life, my beloved Isa."

168

Lisa's eyes teared up. She nodded. Her father got up from the sofa and picked up their empty mugs.

"Well, off to bed now," he said. "You're going to need a good night's sleep if you're going to save the world."

"You have no idea," Lisa said and squeezed his shoulder. When she looked into his eyes, so like her own, she saw something she hadn't seen in a long time.

Hope.

## 29

*I have looked into Garnok's eye . . .*

Linda staggered out of bed. Fumbling, only half-awake, she
followed the voice that called to her. But the metallic voice faded
and disappeared as she looked around her darkened bedroom.
Her pajama-clad legs shook against the wood floor where a
few strips of dawn light had found their way in through gaps in
the blinds.

She finally understood now, but she needed help to be able to
see everything. Things still slipped away from her, back into the
darkness. Was it too early to text the others? She felt around on
her nightstand where she usually kept her eyeglasses. Surely they
were there? She groped around more, still not finding her glasses,
but almost tipping a half-full glass of water over onto a thick
paperback.

"Mornings," she mumbled. "Who needs them?"

Misty yawned widely and seemed to agree. Her green eyes
glowed in the semi-darkness.

Finally, Linda had her phone in her hand and her eyeglasses
on—they had been resting on the windowsill. It was a quarter to
six in the morning. Who else would be awake this early?

She thought she knew.

Alex answered on the second ring. She sounded perky, as if she had been up for a while already. Linda could hear a scraping sound and a muffled whinny in the background.

"Are you at the stables?" Linda asked, smiling to herself. Just as she had expected.

"Obviously," Alex replied, leaning her shovel against the wall. "I'm mucking out stalls. What about you? What are you doing up this early? School is canceled, you know. And we decided that we aren't going riding until after breakfast, right? Or did I miss something?"

"I need your help," Linda hurriedly said. "You have to come here and help me get everything out of my head, like you did before. Can you call Anne and ask her to call Lisa? Come here, all three of you, as soon as you can. I'm making breakfast and then we'll leave."

"Give me five minutes."

"Thank you," Linda said. But Alex had already hung up.

An hour later, all four of them were sitting on Linda's hastily made bed. Misty, who refused to leave Linda, was curled up on her lap. Her gentle purring had a soothing effect, even now.

She scratched the little black cat under the chin. Then she took a deep breath and looked up. Three curious pairs of eyes stared back at her. Lisa's hair was even more disheveled than normal, and Anne had yawned almost as many times as Misty, but suddenly all their tiredness was blown away. Everyone was quiet, waiting. Linda realized that they were all waiting for her to say something, to guide them into the unknown.

What on Earth should she say?

"Okay," she said finally. "You remember how we did this last time, right? In the druids' house at the Secret Stone Circle, you helped me bring the images into focus. That's how we realized that the dam was going to burst. We have to do the same thing again now. Focusing is the most important thing. Now, hold hands and close your eyes. Don't open your eyes until I say so. And whatever you do, don't let go!"

Linda's left temple throbbed dully. She rubbed it, as if she were just going to physically pull the images out of her head. That was a bit like how it felt, actually. She pictured a closed box that she had to pry open, carefully and cunningly. She felt the heat from Alex and Anne, who were sitting close to her. She heard their regular, calm breathing. The mattress squeaked as someone—could that be Lisa?—squirmed a little. Everyone had their eyes closed, but it was still possible to perceive light coming from outside the bedroom window, like a faint glimmer through their closed eyelids.

And then everything was dark. And cold. Linda squeezed her friends' hands, feeling them squeeze back.

She saw. And her friends saw what she saw. It was almost like a movie, although Linda was broadcasting it straight into their brains. She was the director and they were the audience.

At first it was hard to see anything beyond the black ocean, the rolling waves, and the infinitely dark sky. But there was something floating in the water, something that didn't belong out here, an intruder quietly gliding through the night. All four of them had seen it in another form, moored in the harbor. Now Dark Core Headquarters was drifting around, way out at sea. No land as far as the eye could see.

A fierce wind churned the water, the night-black water, crashing waves up onto the platform. It glistened like a dark gem on the cold deck.

Linda gasped for air as she tried to zoom in. Her head throbbed. It felt just like the beginning of a migraine. The nighttime blackness flickered. For a brief instant, fresh October morning light fell over the dark platform.

"Come on now," Linda mumbled. "Stay with me."

A bolt of lightning struck the shadow-shrouded platform. After that, a star lit up in the sky, bright like a lighthouse. A faint glimpse of the sun appeared for a brief instant right beside it.

"Thank you," Linda whispered to her friends.

She kept her eyes closed, zooming in further still. They glided closer to the strange machine and recognized it. And they recognized the man standing beside it. His pale face was covered in shiny red scars and he was moving even more stiffly than before. But it was him.

John Sands. His sharp teeth gleamed in the night as he reached his hand out toward something dark, glossy, and muddy, which could just be made out in the middle of the portal. His eyes were bulging, open wide, his face filled with rapture and bliss.

It was like the birth of a monster.

*Sick*, Alex thought with a shudder. But she made sure to stay in the moment, keeping her eyes shut tight.

They had to stick with it, this unimaginable image they were seeing in Linda's vision. Evil was coming to Jorvik. Garnok was being liberated.

What they were seeing must never come to pass.

Never.


Zooming in once more, a new headache. Linda was starting to get fatigued now, but she clung tenaciously to the dark vision. Her friends helped her persevere, despite the pain. Just having them sitting there right beside her, sharing the visions, helped.

Alex held her one hand, which started to sear in pain. Anne shrank back as she felt something slimy and serpent-like grab her.

She didn't want to be dragged in. She had to stay out. But soon, she realized, the darkness was going to take her hand. She would have to be ready soon. She shivered.

Something wriggly, glistening, and black, like wet tree roots, could be made out below the surface of the frothy waters. A bony hand reached out and fumbled after the wriggling thing.

"Garnok," Mr. Sands said over and over again. "You're here now. Finally, you're here!"

Linda's head was practically vibrating inside now. She put her hand to her forehead, forcing herself to focus. They had to get down to the ocean. There was something there they had to see.

Linda's vision continued down beneath the water's surface. It moved quickly, like a roller coaster. Far below, on the ocean floor, pink cracks gleamed. The light from the cracks was blinding, disco-strength. Now everything was black and pink, pink and black. The ocean roared and bubbled in time with Mr. Sands's disjointed squawks of delight.

Linda fell backward with a stifled cry. She opened her eyes the instant her head landed on the pillow.

"There," she half-whispered. "You can look again."

At first there was complete silence. Linda rubbed her temples as her intense headache receded. Then she said, "I really thought my head would explode. Did you guys see?"

"Yes," Anne said, but her eyes said something else. They said, *No, why, how?* They said, *I'm scared.*

They said the exact same thing that Linda's eyes did.

Alex got up off the bed and started pacing. Her eyes were wide with a wild look.

"Would you quit walking around? I'm nervous enough as is!" Lisa exclaimed, looking annoyed.

"You don't think I am?!" Alex blurted out. But she stopped pacing and sat down at Linda's desk instead. She restlessly picked up a pen and started playing with it.

"We have to remember one thing now," Linda said. Her voice was finally working again. "What we saw . . . that doesn't have to happen. Like with the dam, I saw the worst-case scenario, not what would have happened if we managed to mend the dam. What we saw just now is *one* possible outcome. Mr. Sands frees Garnok using the portal and the cracks. That can't happen. That *won't* happen. Because we are not going to let it happen!"

"How did he even get out of that portal?" Alex asked, dropping the pen so that it spun away across the desktop. "Concorde kicked him into it."

"I don't know," Linda replied. "But somehow he managed to make his way back out. The druids have sensed his presence the whole time. Maybe he was just licking his wounds. Nothing seems to be able to stop that madman. And apparently he's found a way to set Garnok free. We have to stop him. We have to stop Garnok, once and for all. It's our only hope."

"But how?" Anne's voice was scarcely more than a whisper.

"By doing the same thing we did in the Light Ceremony," Linda replied. "We did it once. We can do it again."

"An overflowing dam feels like a pretty minimal task compared to a monster," Alex muttered. Her hand still burned.

"I'm scared, too," Linda said, looking Alex straight in the eye. "But we have to do this."

"Uh, who said anything about being scared?" Alex responded dismissively. "You mentioned breakfast earlier. I'm starving."

"And we need to pack, too," Lisa reminded them. "Before the ride. Just the bare necessities, right? Just what we need to save the world. I'm thinking we should travel light."

"Always good to pack light for the apocalypse," Alex agreed with a smile.

Linda laughed and got up to go fetch tea and toast from the kitchen. Once she returned with a fully loaded tray and everyone had dug in, she said, "I think that sounds like a good idea, Lisa. We'll pack what we need, then we'll set out. And then we'll try to get Fripp and the druids to tell us more about what's actually going on. Together we'll find out where Mr. Sands is searching for Garnok. We'll find him. And then . . . then we'll go there. Right into the darkness. Somehow."

The air felt stifling, but not from their steaming mugs of tea. As the reality of what they needed to do sank in, the seriousness of it all hit them, almost palpably. One by one they nodded.

"Watch out, darkness," Alex said. "We're coming for you."

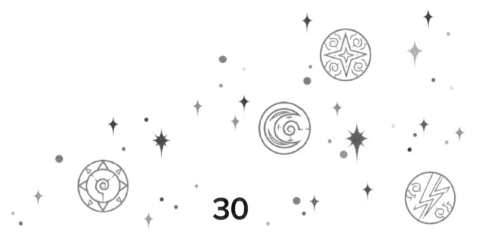

# 30

"Aren't you going to ask if we're almost there yet, Alex?" Linda's voice was teasing but warm as she turned around in her saddle and smiled at her friend.

"Ha ha," Alex responded. "Very funny."

They had made it a long way up into the Northern Mountain Range, but they had a long way to go before they reached the Secret Stone Circle. Every minute felt like hours now as the storm raged above them like cold, gray lashes from a whip. They rode as closely together as possible, both to keep warm by drafting off of each other and to block some of the icy winds. At the same time, they rode close together because they needed to be close to each other now.

*If this were a play, the curtains would go up now for the final act,* Linda thought. *What we're about to do will determine the future—our future and Jorvik's future. Maybe even the world's. No pressure.*

Out loud she said, "Can we talk about something totally different for a while, you guys? I want to hear that there's going to be an *after*. What are you going to do afterward, Lisa, once all of this is over and we don't need to worry about Garnok and Mr. Sands anymore?"

"Well . . ." Lisa said, drawing it out as she ducked to avoid a branch. "First of all, I'm going to try to stay here in Jorvik. My dad has started talking about moving away from Jorvik because it's too dangerous here."

"WHAT?!" the other girls exclaimed in unison.

Alex slumped in her saddle, so dramatically that Tin-Can whinnied in protest.

"Seriously, Lisa," Alex objected. "He can't do that! You *have* to stay here. He needs to understand that!"

"I know," Lisa nodded. "And I think he gets it. I had a long talk with him last night, actually, after I got home from the stables. He said that he was going to let me do what I need to do, that he trusts me."

"Does he know that you're a Soul Rider?" Linda wondered.

"Um, I don't know," Lisa said with a shrug. "I don't think he knows that there's a name for it. But after what happened on the platform, he gets that I—we—are involved in something magical and dangerous. And he understood that he had to let me come with you guys now. But . . . I don't know what it will be like later, you know, after the storm. Or, how should I put this? I don't know if I'm going to be able to convince him that we need to stay here in Jorvik after everything that's happened."

She stopped talking. She stroked Starshine's silky, freshly groomed coat, touching his blue mane as it blew in the wind.

"So anyway, I applied to music school a while ago," Lisa said. "You know, the big, famous one in Jorvik City. I looked into it when I first arrived. Before I met you guys. I should hear back really soon about whether or not I got in for the spring semester. It feels so frivolous to think about that now, when we're not even sure there will BE a spring semester, you know? It's one way to cope, I guess, thinking about the future, focusing on practical things. Plans, life, that kind of thing."

"I totally get it," Linda said, nodding slowly. "I've been doing the same thing. Checking the registration dates for jumping competitions and entering. You have to plan for an afterward, otherwise you'll go crazy."

"Music school, huh?" Alex said with a wry smile. "Oh, they're soooo going to accept you. Although obviously we're going to miss you at school. Good thing we'll still see each other at the stables."

Anne shook her head. It almost looked like she had tears in her eyes.

"I don't care about music school, but—hello—moving?! No! You *have* to talk him out of it, Lisa! You guys have to stay in Jorvik. We can't just go our separate ways, not now, not ever."

"Exactly," Linda said. Alex nodded. She was looking down at Tin-Can's bushy mane so that it was hard to make eye contact with her. But Lisa thought her eyes looked teary.

"Even if you stay in Jorvik, you're going to go to music school, probably this spring already. We won't see each other at school anymore. It won't be the same," Alex said dully.

"You don't need to see each other every day at school to be best friends," Anne said quickly, her eyes wandering. "Haven't you heard that saying? 'Good friends are like stars. You don't always see them—but you know they're always there.'"

"What does that mean?" Alex said.

"Um," Anne said, slowing down slightly. "I need to tell you guys something, too. I got into a dressage school and I'm going to start next semester. It's pretty far outside of Jorvik City, close to our house. And I get to bring Concorde. They have a spot for him in the stables."

Alex was heartbroken. She hoped that the disappointment wasn't too visible on her face when she said, "It'll be so great for

179

you to not have to commute back and forth between Jorvik City and Jarlaheim anymore. And dressage school, that's so cool! Promise you won't forget us when you're competing for Jorvik in the Olympics."

"Never," Anne laughed. "I would never forget you! Not for as long as I live. And, you guys, stop looking so mopey! We're going to see each other all the time. The last time I checked, Jorvik City was still located in Jorvik."

"So, Linda . . . ?" Alex sounded dubious. "Are you about to tell us you got into some obscure boarding school for geniuses on the other side of the island?"

It was Linda's turn to laugh now.

"I wish!" Linda said. "No way, Alex. You won't get rid of me that easily. We're still going to be classmates, you and me. How would it look if we all bailed right after we succeeded in saving the world?"

"Assuming we succeed, that is," Anne interjected.

"Right," Linda replied. "Assuming that we succeed."

For a while, only the storm and the persistent shrieks of a wild horse down in the valley below could be heard. Alex's hand tingled. She thought about the lightning that would come soon, her lightning, summoned using a power she didn't fully understand how to wield yet. Even though she had seen Linda's vision and had felt Garnok's presence as an intense pain in her hand and in her head, it was so hard to know what would happen when the time came.

But she did know one thing. When the time came, she would have her friends with her. She wiped a tear from her cheek and cleared her throat. A blackbird chirped its beautiful, lonely song from the top of a swaying pine tree. *How could it hold on and sing in this wind?* Alex wondered. *Why wasn't it quiet?*

She knew why. The blackbird sang because it had to. Just like she and the others had to keep riding, straight into something so big and dangerous that there were hardly words for it. Maybe the right words could be found in one of the scary suspense books that Linda loved to read, but Alex had no words. Still, when she heard that little blackbird singing through the storm, it was like it released something inside her anyway.

Far, far away she could sense the long, serpentine path that would carry them up to the Secret Stone Circle. Alex urged Tin-Can along, then she called to the others: "Come on! Here we go! The druids are waiting for us."

And behind her, her friends matched her feverish pace.

## 31

"By Aideen's Light, the darkness is close now!"

Fripp's big, black eyes were wide. Elizabeth and the other druids were gathered around him, motionless and grim in their gray cloaks. Lisa looked around and sensed the seriousness of the moment. The sun shone weakly, creating a sheer reflection that danced across the grass. The girls were startled. How long had it been since they had seen the sun? Days, at least. As was so often the case, the weather was nicer at the Secret Stone Circle than in other places on the island. The magic of the stone circle kept the storm at bay, and the sun shone defiantly on the runestones.

Now and then, some of the ancient inscriptions shimmered a little extra, like shooting stars.

They had finally arrived. The storm they had just ridden through at a full gallop still howled in their ears. They needed to act quickly now. If only Fripp would hurry up . . .

But no, he started to talk about the cosmos again now.

One of the older druids joined in and began chanting slowly. After what felt like at least an hour, the older druid looked up with a somber expression and said, "The signs are here. The time is now. Even so, I ask that you try to stay calm, Soul Riders. Acting prematurely"—the druid looked sternly at Linda, who was desperately trying to stifle a yawn— "is not something that the Keepers of

Aideen endorse. Quite the contrary: impulsive acts can have serious consequences. We have already seen this. So, we druids request self-control yet again. With the help of the stars and the runic texts, we will find the right solution. And soon. Fripp, what do the maps say?"

The small blue creature started rustling his old papers again. If he only wore eyeglasses, he would look like a comical version of Santa Claus reading children's wish lists, Lisa thought, suppressing a giggle.

Alex sighed loudly. Anne clomped restlessly back and forth like a bored circus horse. Her high, blond ponytail bobbed as she moved.

Linda was at least as impatient as her friends, but a small part of her wished that they weren't there at all. *It would be so nice to not be here right now. To not need to hunt for a monster and feel like everything was coming to an end. To just sit home with Misty and read about other people's adventures, fictional adventures.*

But there was no point in thinking like that. So, she pushed those thoughts aside and focused on Fripp instead. Could he help them find an exact position? Could they find out where Mr. Sands and the headquarters were going?

They knew one thing: wherever Mr. Sands was going, that's where Garnok was. And Garnok must not be released. If that happened, then the world they all lived in and took for granted might come to an end. No more rides in the woods and happy laughter, no music, no warmth and goodness. No spring flowers to pick on a sunny May day.

The storm was only the beginning. It could get so much worse, *would* get so much worse—if the Soul Riders couldn't stop it.

When you stood at the Secret Stone Circle, surrounded by so much mystery and history, it was easy to start thinking of how short a human life was, how many people had lived throughout history, compared to everyone who was alive right then. Lisa had thought about that several times in just that spot. But the fact that everything might soon be coming to an end, all of it, *now?* It was inconceivable. It was impossible to grasp, even then as they watched all the adults' furrowed brows and anxious looks.

"Have you found anything?" Linda wondered, leaning closer to Fripp. He just mumbled in response and kept examining the old maps.

There wasn't much that moved quickly in Fripp's world, but that's presumably how it was when you were immortal, Linda thought, sighing to herself. Although if he had ever felt like picking up the pace a little, this would have been the ideal time for it.

Fripp's full attention was focused on the maps he held in his hand. They appeared to have been made on some thicker type of paper—maybe parchment?—and they emitted a heavy, musty scent of time gone by. They must have been several centuries old. Although if they knew Fripp at all, it was probably more like millennia. As Fripp browsed through the maps, the pages crinkled and rustled. Anne peeked over his shoulder, curious. She was so tall, and he was so short, that she had to kneel down to see properly. She could see coordinates and place names on the yellowing paper, but also various symbols, including the star, moon, lightning, and sun.

"Are those us, Fripp? Are those Soul Riders?" She grinned and pointed. "Ouch!" she yelled when the little creature with the blue fur smacked her fingers with his hairy paw.

"No one beside me can touch these maps!" he said in a stern voice. "They're priceless!"

"So are we," Alex mumbled, so quietly that only her friends could hear what she said. Although when she looked up, she saw that Elizabeth was also chuckling.

Okay. She had heard her, too. Most definitely.

At first, Fripp only muttered in response. He was staring at some pink cracks that ran right through the map. Lisa stared, too.

"Wait," she said breathlessly. "Those cracks weren't there on the map a second ago. How . . . ?"

"These maps were drawn hundreds of years ago," Fripp said with an almost dream-like expression on his alert, squirrel-like face. "But as I'm sure you understand, these are not normal maps. They constantly redraw themselves, since they are directly linked to the Pandorian flow. So, what you see here"—he waved a paw over an area of the map covered with glowing pink cracks—"are the Pandorian cracks that have arisen in the ocean."

Fripp squinted and carefully traced the cracks across the map with his paw.

"The cracks are definitely too big be to be natural. In all likelihood, it was Mr. Sands's portal that caused them. The portal rips open wounds between the worlds, releasing energy to flow between Pandoria and our world. We can already see that in the storm raging around us."

The little blue creature looked up and blinked his big eyes.

"Soul Riders," Fripp said, "you were right. The portal has already created big enough cracks that Garnok could certainly manage to break free. These cracks must be closed!"

"We KNEW we were right!" Lisa interrupted. "That's exactly what we were trying to say before the druids started babbling— sorry, *talking!*"

Avalon and the other druids looked at her in annoyance. She didn't let that silence her.

"Fripp? Elizabeth? Avalon? Anyone, hello?" Lisa continued. "We need to do something NOW, not later. Because otherwise there might not be any later. And if you have any suggestions for what we should do, we would be really happy to hear them. Like, now. I know that you've had a bunch of secret meetings and that you've discussed how we're going to resolve this. So, if you have any ideas that could help us, please say so. *Now.*"

One by one they shook their heads. Alex sighed.

"Great," she said. "No suggestions. Why did we even ride all the way here if we have to handle everything on our own anyway?"

"Listen up, girls." Elizabeth's gentle voice was a sharp contrast to Alex's hard, tense one. "Never believe that we don't want to help you. There is nothing we want more, but the Pandorian glare right now is so strong that it's blocking everything. We can't even think properly. I suggest that we go rest and try again a little later. We just need the very last piece of the puzzle. We're almost there. So bear with us, don't give up now!" she added with a smile. "We can do this."

"How do you know that?" Alex asked. Her voice sounded a little less sharp now.

"I just do," Elizabeth replied. "Alex, do you trust me?"

"You know I do," Alex whispered. "Always."

"Good. Now make sure that you trust yourselves just as much. Because you're going to need your Soul Rider instincts. Soon."

The druids bowed slightly to Fripp, and then they left.

"Thanks for nothing, then!" Alex yelled right out loud as the druids and Fripp slowly wandered off in a somber huddle of grayish-blue.

# 32

After the druids and Fripp left, the girls remained, their heads drooping. They noticed that the runestones, which usually glowed pink, looked sad and gray under the heavy clouds. It felt as if the air had gone out of the Secret Stone Circle.

"They don't get it!" Linda exclaimed. "This is a matter of life and death! If we wait, there might not be any Secret Stone Circle left anymore, no Jorvik! There's not much time, and they still want us to wait. I can't believe it!"

"At least we have Elizabeth. She understands the situation," Alex said, once the druids were out of earshot. "She'll help us no matter what."

"Yeah, she will. But it would have been nice if the other druids were a little more upbeat and helpful, too," Linda replied.

Lisa patted Starshine, who was anxiously looking back and forth between the girls. Her free hand was clenched into a tight, angry fist. Linda hadn't seen her this angry since they had spent the night in the woods, arguing about rescuing her father. Lisa's arm muscles flexed as she spoke.

"I think this is all super unfair. We were the ones who made sure to kick Mr. Sands into that machine! Evil begone, *POOF!* Isn't that what we were supposed to do: defend Jorvik from evil? Well, we did that, and we rescued my dad, too. And what do we get in return? A bunch of bellyaching! I'd like to see Avalon stand up to Mr. Sands and that terrible machine," she muttered. "It's pretty safe to just sit up here in the mountains, isn't it? They even have *sunshine* up here, since they're almost completely protected from the storm! Sure, they can sit up here with their runes and talk about how important it is to *weigh all the various angles*. What other angles are there to consider, anyway?! Either we do something—or everything is doomed. It's as simple as that."

Lisa's words resonated in Linda. For so many years she had read about other people's exploits, taking inspiration and strength from different role models. Now it was her—their—turn to step up and act. She knew that they couldn't wait any longer. Even so, her knees trembled as she sat down by the runestone. Anne sat next to her, lost in her own thoughts.

"What do you think, Anne?" Linda asked.

The words stuck in Anne's throat. Even so, she had to say them out loud.

"Yes, well . . ." she began uncertainly. Then, with a passion that almost startled the others, she said, "You get that the druids are a little bit right, too, don't you? About certain things, in any case. We have been extremely careless with the magic. And we can't plan our way out of a paper bag. The fact that Mr. Sands fell into the portal when we rescued Lisa's dad, that was hardly thanks to us. Concorde did that and it was pure luck. If he hadn't kicked Mr. Sands right when he did, we'd likely all be prisoners now. Or worse. And we would never get to see our horses again."

Anne turned to look at Concorde, who was lying in the grass a little way off, resting. His eyes were moving around under his closed eyelids and she wondered if he was dreaming. She hoped it was a nice dream.

"I don't regret anything we've done," Anne continued. "Just the opposite. I don't really believe in regretting anything anymore. It's just silly to do that. And Lisa got her father back in the end. So, it was worth it, no matter how tough it was afterward with the horses and everything. But the druids have a point when they say that we need to learn to control ourselves before we set out. I'm sorry, but they *do*. I don't know what earlier Soul Riders were like or what methods they used. But in all honesty, there's just no way that they can have been as disorganized as we are. If they were, Jorvik wouldn't be here today. You guys must see how we're just sort of plowing ahead."

She looked around at her friends, who were listening in silence, and then she took a deep breath and continued.

"So far, it's worked out for us, but what do we do now?" Anne continued. "We know that Garnok will get out soon. If that happens, it might be the end of Jorvik and the *Earth*. We know that we have to seal the cracks again to stop that from happening. But we don't know where they are or how we get there."

"Okay, you're right," Alex mumbled. She was holding a crumbly autumn leaf in one hand. Her eyes were big and shiny as she continued. "I agree with you that the druids are crazy slow. I can't cope with any more waiting, but to just set out again . . . you realize how lucky we've been to stay alive this far, right? How will we survive the awful *Garnok* if we're not prepared and we don't know where we're going?"

Everyone was looking down at the ground. A rune sparkled pink and purple before it turned gray and cold again.

"Well, so what's the answer then?" Lisa wondered grumpily. "What, should we start our own order or something, without the druids? Maybe Linda should be keeping minutes for this meeting?"

"Ugh, stop goofing around," Linda said. "You know perfectly well what Anne and Alex mean."

"Yeah, I do," Lisa replied hesitantly. "But I still think it's super unfair that the druids had the nerve to *complain* about us taking some initiative, like we did up at the dam and with my father. It's not like they were super clear about what was going on."

"No, they really weren't," Linda sighed.

Anne perked up her ears. Suddenly she heard hushed voices from inside Fripp's burrow. She nodded.

"Look, it sounds like they're going to be busy for a while longer. Come on, let's go do some training so we're ready now rather than *later!*"

And soon, all four of them were standing around the rune-stones again. They had noticed that sometimes when you don't know what to do and everything feels hopeless, it feels nice to keep busy. So, they practiced the Light Ceremony and their magic in the hopes that those Soul Rider instincts Elizabeth had mentioned would come alive in them. On that gloomy, windy day, the lightning and the sunshine competed with each other. Anne caught a sunbeam, inhaled, and focused. Then she let it go at full force. The smell of burnt grass lay thick over the Secret Stone Circle. They kept working. Time passed. The heavy clouds glowed with a faint, pink light.

"Let's pretend that's Garnok right there," Alex said, pointing at the burning clump of grass. Linda used the coolness of the moon to put out the fire, while Lisa healed the grass so that it regained its lush, green splendor.

"Well done, you guys," Anne nodded. "How about a break? We've been practicing for hours now."

The others nodded.

"The druids still seem to be gathered at Fripp's place," Linda said. "So, we can talk undisturbed for a little while longer anyway."

"Yeah, or for a hundred years if they get things their way," Lisa said. "If the druids don't come up with a plan after lunch, I promise you, I'm going to lose it! And then I'm just going to set out on my own."

"*We'll* set out on our own," Alex corrected. "Enough is enough already!"

From inside the cave they heard agitated voices. Snippets of what they said echoed out and could be heard in the meadow.

*It's time . . .*

*You can't withhold . . .*

*Dangerous to speculate . . .*

*We have to be sure . . .*

*How can we . . .*

*. . . Garnok . . .*

*. . . the great battle . . .*

*. . . although we don't know for sure . . .*

*It's time.*

"Why don't we get to attend those meetings?" Alex said, drinking from a water jug. "After all, we're the ones they're arguing about."

The wind roared below them on the mountainside. It sounded almost like a wounded animal, Linda thought. And maybe it was, she realized, suddenly feeling a chill. From up here they could see more of the wild horses fleeing from the storm, while people tried in vain to capture them.

Suddenly, the girls jumped as a massive, bright pink lightning bolt struck a tree just beyond the entrance to the Secret Stone Circle.

"Things are going downhill fast," Alex said in distress. "We have to deal with this. *Now!*"

Beyond the mountain, there was an alarming rumble. Lisa's heart began to race.

"It's as if the flow from the cracks has grown so strong that not even the Secret Stone Circle's magic can keep it away any longer. Can't you feel it creeping closer and closer?"

"I don't even think we have until nighttime to deal with this anymore," Anne said, looking sadly down at the fleeing horses in the distance. "Maybe not even hours. We need to go now. Come on, let's focus! We need to come up with a plan. For example, how are we going to find the right place? And how do we get there? That feels like the most important thing, so that we can close the cracks and put a stop to Mr. Sands and Garnok. There has to be a way!"

Linda sat down next to Meteor, pulled a little notepad out of her long, gray cardigan, and started writing intently. Meteor looked up at her and nudged her gently with his nose.

"What do you say, buddy?" Linda asked, petting his blaze. "Do you have some brilliant plan?"

Anne and Alex looked at each other. There was a seriousness in their eyes, in this moment, that they could no longer back away from. They mustn't back away, not now.

"It feels like we're disobedient kids and the druids are our parents who can't agree on how they're going to raise us," Anne sighed. "And while we're waiting for them to decide on, well, whatever they're in there discussing right now, we're just waiting out here, treading water. It's so incredibly frustrating! We *know* that Mr. Sands is planning to free Garnok. We *know* it's going to happen soon. How are we supposed to get to the right place and close those cracks? Do you have any ideas, Alex? You're always so resourceful."

Alex sighed. Beyond the runes, very close to the ravine where the wind was raging, a wild rabbit was running around, chasing the purple light from the runestones. Its big, black eyes moved back and forth attentively between the streaks of light. The little cotton tail wagged in step with the eyes.

"Oh, to be that rabbit right now," Alex said. "It has no idea that everything is about to fall apart. It's just chasing the light because it's fun."

"Yeah, I'd love to trade places," said Lisa, who was standing a little way off, lost in thought. "Imagine not having any worries, how nice that would be." She glanced over at Linda, who was still writing feverishly. "Any ideas yet?" she added encouragingly. She hoped, like the others, that Linda would have an idea. She usually did.

But Linda just shook her head.

"Nothing," Linda said. "I've been thinking and thinking and thinking. I feel like my head is going to explode. I've written down a bunch of random facts and thoughts, but I just don't know." She started pacing back and forth. "Yeah, I actually don't know, but *maybe* the druids and Fripp do know. But I guess they have to hold eight big meetings and jabber on and on first. Gah, this is all so frustrating! We are so close, but no one else seems to understand how urgent this is!"

"It's hopeless," Alex said, her shoulders slumping. "And despite all of the lightning I fired off this morning, I still feel zero Soul Rider instinct. Sorry, Elizabeth, but I think you think too highly of us."

The sun shone through the heavy cloud layer and made the runestones light up in shimmering purple hues. A gigantic purple reflection moved across the meadow. The rabbit raced toward it. Then suddenly it was gone. The light, too.

"Where did it go?" Linda said, squinting.

Anne abruptly stood up and walked over to the edge of the ravine, taking long strides.

"Careful!" Lisa yelled. "Don't fall off!"

"I have no intention of falling off," Anne said. Then she squatted down and inspected the tall grass. She lifted a couple of clumps of grass and picked up a small stone. Her eyes were attentive, her eyebrows furrowed.

"What is she doing?" Alex whispered to Lisa. Lisa shrugged and kept watching Anne's movements.

"Aha!" Anne suddenly exclaimed. A second later, the rabbit popped right out of the ground. It stopped and looked at her wide-eyed before scampering along.

"A secret escape route," Anne said, pointing to a tunnel in the ground. "That's why it disappeared. That hole was there all along. We just didn't see it. No, *we just didn't see it* ..." She wiped her hands on her pants and cast one last look at the ground. Then she looked up with a triumphant smile.

"I think I have an idea."

That very moment, a shadow towered behind her.

"What kind of idea are you talking about, girls?"

# 33

Anne stood up and found herself looking into Elizabeth's unwavering gray eyes. Then she looked around at the other Soul Riders.

"There is a way to find Mr. Sands and the Dark Riders," Anne replied. "And I'm not going to pretend that it isn't dangerous. It's risky, but right now it's our only chance so I vote that we take it. Which is to say: there is a way. It's been there the whole time, but we just haven't realized it. Just like the rabbit and the hole in the ground. We take the back way to the cracks, through Pandoria! It will be easier for us to reach both the cracks and Mr. Sands from there. We'll use the Light Ceremony, just like at the dam. And we'll help each other. It *could* actually work!"

"Pandoria?" Alex said skeptically. "Where you and Concorde ended up? That pink nightmare? We're supposed to go there, voluntarily?"

Elizabeth raised her hands in warning.

"Two things," Elizabeth said. "One, that's a good idea. Excellent, Anne, that you thought of that! But, and now I come to point two, what you're talking about doing could potentially be deadly. Pandorian energy is enormously high right now. That's the very energy that Mr. Sands is planning to use to release Garnok. If you go to Pandoria, you will quite literally be in the eye of the storm.

There will be no turning back. I want you guys to understand that. What you set in motion if you go there will not go away again until you have defeated it."

"We understand that," Anne replied quickly. "But I think that this may be our only chance. I mean, look around. Look at those trees down there. They've been completely destroyed by the storm. You KNOW that we have to do this. And we need to do it now. Because if we wait, then there might not be any Jorvik left to fight for."

"I'm glad you understand how dangerous this is," Elizabeth nodded. "But you're right. You have to act now, while there's still time. We can't hold you back any longer. And using Pandoria might not be a bad idea. Anne has been there before and can find her way around. She can guide you, with help from the Path of the Winds and your collective magical powers." She grew somber again as she looked at them. "And you're right: it has to happen now. Garnok has been imprisoned for millennia. Through generation after generation of Soul Riders and druids, he has tried to find an ally who could release him. He has one now in Mr. Sands. When he stole the energy from your horses, Mr. Sands obtained the energy necessary to release Garnok. The storm, the island that feels like it's coming apart, the ocean . . . they're all signs that he is close to succeeding."

Alex glanced at Lisa, who suddenly looked very guilty. Lisa's words tumbled out of her mouth as she said, "So, this was all triggered by us taking our horses to Dark Core Headquarters to rescue my father?"

Elizabeth looked into Lisa's worried eyes with her own calm ones.

"You mustn't believe that this is your fault. It would have happened sooner or later anyway, Lisa. And pointing fingers or thinking about everything that could have been different doesn't help at all. The only thing that matters now is what we do about it. We have to stop Mr. Sands from releasing Garnok. I know you girls can do it!"

Linda felt how Elizabeth's words made her feel warm inside, but she didn't know if she dared to believe what Elizabeth had said. She took a deep breath.

"How do we find the cracks once we get to Pandoria?" Linda asked.

"In our world, the cracks are pink because Pandoria's unreality leaks out through them," Elizabeth responded. "In Pandoria, the cracks are green. You'll follow the green light. Once you've found them, you have to perform the Light Ceremony. If you manage to close the cracks, then the portal's energy will be cut off and, judging from the strength of the storm, Mr. Sands must have already used all the power that the portal stole from your horses. So, if you succeed, this is the end for Mr. Sands. But ..." Elizabeth quietly cleared her throat. "It's going to be a lot harder than at the dam. I believe in you. You're our only hope."

Alex gulped noisily.

"Follow the green light," Anne repeated. There was a thoughtful look in her blue eyes.

"Exactly," Elizabeth nodded. "And it must be done now."

"Now as in *now?*" Alex exclaimed. That sounded drastic. Even so, she knew that it wasn't soon enough.

They needed to get to Pandoria on the double, because soon it would be too late. Too late for them—and maybe for all of Jorvik.

## 34

The storm swirled uncontrollably around them as they prepared to depart. They hurriedly mounted their horses, teetering in the wind that not even the Secret Stone Circle's multiple millennia's worth of magic could hold off any longer. The sky was one dark, desperate omen. Even the runestones seemed to have darkened, losing their shimmer.

The druids' long cloaks flapped in the wind and made them look like large birds. In other circumstances, Alex would have laughed. She wasn't laughing now. Her usually animated face was pale and silent as she stroked Tin-Can's neck. Tin-Can's coat, long and yellow like his mane, was ruffled by the wind.

A flock of robins flew across the sky, close together, their wings wavering in the wind. Lisa looked around. She leaned over to Alex and whispered, "There are so many of them—the druids, I mean. Almost as many of them as those birds over there. As if they had gathered here, flocked together, away from the storm and the evil."

"Another huge group of them just arrived," Alex said with a nod. "Of druids, I mean. I hope they didn't come here un-necessarily."

Avalon and Elizabeth stepped forward, regarding the four young girls with somber, subdued faces. Fripp stood next to them;

he was small compared to all the druids. He was silent. *It isn't like him to be silent,* Lisa thought.

But then again, nothing seemed normal right now. They could feel the seriousness and weight of the moment so intensely. They cowered before it. In the distance, they saw a hazy red glow. Something was burning in the forest down below. Lisa gulped and turned to Elizabeth.

"I'll be thinking about you," Elizabeth said and kissed them on the cheek, one by one. "I'll be thinking about you the whole time."

"And we'll be thinking about you," Linda replied, trying to smile. Her face felt tight, from the wind and from the smile that didn't want to come. She nodded to the druids and started walking away on Meteor, over toward the cliff where the Path of the Winds took off. Anne followed, and then Lisa and Alex. Fripp stood there among the runestones and watched them.

When they reached the cliff's edge, they stopped. They permitted themselves to wait for just a brief moment. They looked down the steep mountainside, at Jorvik which lay below them.

If everything went according to plan, good would prevail. If they failed, evil would win. It was so simple—and so indescribably hard.

"So . . . now we save the world," Lisa said. "No biggie."

"Right, no big deal," Alex agreed. "Totally normal, nothing to see here."

A bolt of lightning raced across the sky and took out an enormous tree just down the slope from them. In the oppressive silence that arose, Linda hesitantly said, "We'll be in another world soon. Have you guys thought about that?"

"Okay, one thing. You can't measure time the same way we do here when you're in Pandoria," Anne said. "All of that belongs to our world. It's irrelevant there."

"Hey, Anne," Lisa said, cocking her head. "You were in Pandoria before. What else can you tell us about it? What's it like there?"

Everyone looked eagerly to Anne, waiting. Tin-Can flattened his ears back in the cold, unpleasant wind. The girls listened attentively, trying to imagine the storm away so that Anne's words came into focus.

"Pandoria can't really be described," she said slowly. "Sure, I can tell you that it's pink, that it feels like being on a really fast carousel that will never stop spinning. I can tell you about pink, vine-like plants that sort of *beckon* you, like some kind of sick hypnosis. I could tell you all of that and a bunch of other stuff. But the thing is that it wouldn't help. You have to be there. You have to experience it for yourself. When we get there, I promise that I'll go in front and show you the way. But until then ... you'll just have to wait and see. You'll know soon enough. The most important thing is that we stick together, like our horse BFFs. Just like they lean on each other when they sleep back home in the pasture, we need to be like that, too. Once we get to Pandoria ... everything is going to be different. Things that we take for granted may suddenly feel wrong. It's so easy to start questioning everything. That's exactly what Pandoria and the unreality there want to happen. But remember, we *have* to stick together. Getting separated would be the worst thing that could happen."

"That's not going to happen," Alex said. She was sitting up quite straight on Tin-Can. Something about her posture and her look of determination made Anne think of a soldier. *Maybe that's what we are*, she thought, *soldiers. But at least we know which side we're fighting for.*

"No," Anne said. She was also sitting up very straight in her saddle now. She was intensely aware of every muscle in her body and the proud beat of her heart: *thump, thump, thump.* "We stand united," Anne said hoarsely. "Now, later, and forever."

She reached out her hand and placed it over Alex's tan, slender hand. Quickly, without hesitating, Linda put her hand on top of Anne's on the other side. Lisa did the same to Linda's. Then, in unison, their voices cracking slightly at this momentous moment, they said: "Now, later, and forever."

They looked at each other for a long time. Then they let go and stepped forward.

# 35

A long time ago, not so long after the island of Jorvik began, four young women rode along a steep, rocky trail. The trail gave way to a forest glade where runestones gleamed in the sunset. Beyond the glade and the hidden circle of stones, the world as they knew it suddenly ended. What remained of their world was only one sheer, steep slope, where the precipice opened up. After that: infinity.

The young riders had been forced to choose: turn back—or continue forward, straight down the cliff. It might seem like a simple choice. Who would deliberately ride off a cliff to a certain death?

But, of course, it was no ordinary cliff. Here—right between the two worlds, where reality frayed and cracked, forming rips like in an old quilt—the abyss didn't mean the end. It was meant to be a beginning instead. It was said that those who ride the Path of the Winds with a pure heart and noble intentions can fly through the air, over the cliff and into Pandoria. Many have tried. Few have succeeded.

The young riders joined hands and closed their eyes, feeling the air move like a gentle breeze. They looked at each other and smiled through their tears. It was now or never. Keep going or give up.

They kept going, right into another world.

Those riders were the first Soul Riders, the first sisterhood. Now, the last sisterhood was riding the same path. Anne rode in the lead, with Concorde's gray mane fluttering in the wind. She told the others not to look down, not to be afraid. They would carry each other the whole way to Pandoria, over the rock ledge and all the way to the other side, rippling through time and space, in one single, gasping breath.

"It's okay to close your eyes," Anne said. "That's what I did. Stay close to me now as I create the portal. Then we take the step."

"See you on the other side," Lisa said, looking Anne straight in the eye. Then she closed her eyes.

Then they all stepped out, all four of them in close, close succession.

Of course, it was magic, ancient magic that has existed for millennia. But it was more than magic. It didn't matter how many spells you knew if you didn't have what the four Soul Riders have.

Each other, today and always.

Over at the Secret Stone Circle, Fripp stood up on a rock ledge and waved to the girls as they flew through the air on their horses. It looked like he was smiling.

# 36

It is said that all actions have consequences and that's probably true. But sometimes things happen that are so big and so important that the consequences are felt far beyond our own world. These events can never be revoked. They are irreversible.

As the Soul Riders tumbled through time and space with their horses, past the Path of the Winds, the storm that had pummeled Jorvik's coast swept over Pandoria. Heavy, dark-purple clouds descended over the cliffs. Winding, neon-pink sea plants were ripped out and flung up on shore. The wind was a deep, wildly angry war cry.

On the Dark Core platform, John Sands stood at the ready. Sabine, Jessica, and Katja stood with their backs to each other, staring out at the furious waters.

Sabine's long braid fluttered in the strong wind. From inside the burning machine, Garnok lured her closer. As if hypnotized, she turned her eyes in his direction. The fire and the darkness flickered, and for a brief second, other images made their way in. Four young women. Four horses. The Path of the Winds and after that, Pandoria.

It startled her.

"I think they're already there. We can't wait any longer now!"

Without looking around for the others, she took a big step, becoming one with the machine's eerie flame and noise. Jessica and Katja followed.

# 37

*Anne was right,* Linda thought when she looked up. There was no way to prepare for Pandoria. You had to experience it for yourself. She blinked her gritty, heavy eyes suspiciously. It felt like she had just woken up from a deep, dreamless sleep.

She saw pink sand dunes around her, pink sand swirling around in the heavy winds. Bright pink, surging water crashed over the shifting purple rocks. It looked kind of like her old Barbie house had just vomited over an entire dimension.

Some distance away, Lisa was trying to stand up. Her legs were unsteady, like a newborn foal's. Linda hadn't tried to stand up yet. She was so dizzy she didn't dare attempt it. Soon . . . she would try soon. Her thoughts were slow and lazy, all jumbled up and recurring. She rested her cheek against the rough ground and drew the air into her lungs. She tried to detect a smell, for surely Pandoria must smell like something.

*Everything smells like something,* she thought.

But she couldn't detect anything: no whiff of ocean, no cold, crispy puff of fresh air. Pandoria, whatever it was, seemed to be odorless. That realization made her uncomfortable.

*We're not in Jorvik anymore, Meteor.*

"Anne! Over here!"

Linda had to yell to be heard over the wind. She was still lying motionless on the ground, as defenseless as a beetle on its back. She didn't think she dared move, not yet. Everything beneath her and around her was an intense, pulsating pink. There was wind causing tempestuous, cherry-colored waves. Green cracks could be made out here and there. A clicking, crunching sound seemed to be coming from the cracks. It reminded Linda of the sound of an egg hatching.

They had done it. They were in Pandoria. It didn't really feel like anything special. Maybe that was the shock. Maybe their sensations hadn't caught up yet. After all, they had traveled between worlds. But Linda guessed she had been expecting to feel more right away.

"I'm coming!" Anne yelled back, the storm whipping her hair back and forth. She was the only one of the four who was still on horseback. Concorde stamped anxiously, puffing out his nostrils. He had been here before, just like Anne. And just like Anne, he knew what a dangerous place Pandoria could be.

And it was more dangerous now than ever before.

"It looks so different," Anne mumbled, looking around. She took in the devastation that surrounded them. Because if they thought that the storm had ravaged Jorvik, that was nothing compared to the sight that met them there. Three of the four of them were encountering Pandoria for the first time, so they had no basis for comparison, no memories, no sites or landmarks to latch onto.

But Anne knew that where a school of pink and purple fish lay gasping for breath now, in the throes of death, there used to be billowing vines in equally brilliant colors. They had slowly and hypnotically swayed their way into her, spreading a kind of calm.

Now those same plants lay before them, dry and withered, ripped out by the ocean and the storm.

Farther out in the water, there was a bubbling, sizzling lightning strike. There were streaks of green, almost like an algae bloom in the ocean which they sometimes had during the hot summers back home in Jorvik. But Anne knew that those were from cracks from our world, coloring the pink water completely green.

"We should have come here sooner." Anne's voice was barely a whisper in the whipping wind.

Linda got to her feet and patted her comfortingly on the arm.

"We couldn't have done anything differently," Linda said. "It was impossible for us to get here until the horses were themselves again."

Anne nodded.

"Stick close to me and the horses now," Anne said. "You might start to feel sick, but it'll pass."

They stood by their horses, so close that they could feel their body heat. The horses saw Concorde's flared nostrils and reacted by backing up, flattening their ears, and scraping with their hooves. Their restless energy was almost palpable.

Lisa pressed herself against Starshine's neck and whispered, "It's all right, buddy. I'm here. We'll be home again soon."

But her voice didn't really carry. It was swallowed up by the wind and her swirling thoughts. She was just as scared as the horses, just as clueless about what was going to happen next.

They led the horses cautiously. The sea was splashing up onto the rocks along the shore. Vines that had been ripped to pieces by the wind and strange, broken shells crunched and snapped under the horses' hooves. Starshine backed away. His eyes were so wide that Lisa could see their whites.

"There, there, buddy," she whispered. "Everything's going to be okay."

"We don't have much time," Anne continued. "Come on!"

They were approaching something that at one time, long ago, had been a temple. A smashed statue lay scattered to the winds outside the magnificent columns. Anne didn't need to get any closer to see who the statue depicted. Curious, Alex hurried over there and saw the contours of a thick, fluffy tail. A pair of shiny black eyes, horribly lifelike even though they were made of glass, stared unseeingly at her as she picked them up out of the ruins.

"Fripp," she whispered. "Here?"

Anne nodded again. They wandered on. Gritty pink sand blew up into their eyes. It became harder and harder to see.

But . . . a little farther in . . . Anne shaded her face, squinting to be able to see clearly. Could that . . . ?

Yes. She turned around and yelled to the others: "Over there! That's where we're going!"

Up ahead, something that appeared to be a round platform rose out of the billowing pink landscape. Something drew Anne toward it. It felt right, as if that was exactly where they needed to be.

*Here it is,* a voice inside her whispered. *This is where it will be decided.*

"Come on," Anne yelled over the gusting wind. "Form a circle around me. There's room for all of us."

They did as she instructed. Suddenly, a dark purple cloud descended over them. The rest of the sky was pink with streaks of emerald green. Anne looked up and thought that she could see the cracks expanding and widening. It was as if the sky itself was turning inside out. She didn't really know if the sound—all the screeching and commotion—was coming from inside the cracks. Maybe it was coming from inside her?

She turned to the others. Pink and green stripes filled her eyes as she began to speak. She blinked vigorously.

"I've already started to feel it," Anne said. "How everything is sort of blending together. I don't know what's me and what's Pandoria anymore. We have to hurry now, before Pandoria's unreality seeps into all of us."

Lisa put her hand over Anne's.

"Here we go," Lisa said, smiling cautiously. "We trust you."

Concorde snorted loudly against Anne's outstretched palm. She stroked his nose quickly. Then she reached one hand up into the air and felt everything that was trying to get in and mess with her inside—the doubt, the uncertainty, the shadow voices—as she struggled to push it away. *Scram*, she thought. The sun shone from above, strong and unrealistically pink.

"Here we go," Anne repeated, feeling the sun's rays warming her from the inside. She let the heat flow out of her hands and up into the sky. For a while she stood totally still, focusing, waiting. Then she saw a thin, gauzy web of tentative little sunbeams emerging around the cracks.

"Look, you guys!" Anne yelled excitedly, pointing.

The ground where they stood trembled and rumbled. Something broke through. At first, they couldn't see what it was. It was big, white, and fumbling. The cracks opened and closed, closed and opened. They heard loud roaring.

"What's going on?" Lisa whispered.

"I don't know," Anne whispered back. As if in a trance, she stared down at the billowing, undulating ground. Something was crawling up out of one of the massive crevices.

Something . . . or *someone*.

Multiple someones.

Linda gasped, blinked, and then found herself staring right into Sabine's face.

"We're here," Sabine said smiling. As Linda looked on in terror, Sabine's eyes glowed, etching themselves into Linda's mind.

# 38

With a smooth tiger's leap, Sabine pounced toward Linda with a loud roar. It was a deep, brutal-sounding roar that sent a shiver straight down Linda's spine.

A battle cry.

An enormous bolt of white lightning cut across the pink sky. Katja stepped out of the bright light. Her horrible white eyes drilled into Lisa's.

"Miss me?" she snarled, grabbing Lisa by the leather jacket. Lisa responded with a horrified gasp.

Staring fiercely at all of them, Jessica took up a broad-legged stance behind Anne and Concorde.

"Mr. Sands?" Linda mumbled, taking in the three Dark Riders and noticing that their leader was missing. "Where's he?"

"He had a guest to look after," Sabine snarled. "If all goes according to plan, his guest will be sticking around for quite a while."

Linda gasped as Sabine slashed deep gashes into her arm. She tensed and prepared mentally for the pain that should have followed. But then she felt the merciful coolness of the moon on her throbbing wounds. She heard Lisa singing and saw the stardust swirling around her.

The gashes were gone, and Linda let the moon she had summoned guide her into battle. *If Sabine is chaos, then I am order,* she managed to think before the power of the Moon Circle took over her.

The extra strength she gained from the moon lasted for a while, but not long enough.

# 39

In our world, a world that may soon be lost, Mr. Sands stood at his portal, somewhere far out at sea, as he had so many times before. He had been waiting for so long—waiting, longing, pleading, and coaxing. Now, finally, the time had come. Yes, now the flames rose high and freezing cold above the thrashing sea. The whole platform shook with the mighty fire that simply grew stronger and stronger. John Sands trembled as well, from both the excitement and the battering winds. The smoke rose black and winding inside the portal, creating menacing patterns in the night sky. The smoke was sometimes black, sometimes pink, and sometimes green. And the contours of a mighty monster emerged within the smoke . . . enormous tentacles, sharp claws, glowing eyes. Mr. Sands stared up at the towering creature in fascination.

"Are you here now, master? Have you finally come?"

Mr. Sands hopped up and down, clapping his hands like an enthusiastic child on his birthday. His face glowed in rapture.

"You are here! Oh, you are here!"

The sky rumbled in response before a giant flash of lightning ripped it in two. The fire was out of control in the portal, blazing out over the entire platform, licking at the concrete floor before heading straight toward Mr. Sands. The fire taunted him as if he were a helpless little rat. Then, the realization shook him, as abruptly as the lightning: Garnok was toying with him.

To Garnok, John Sands was a joke, a means to an end.

His smile suddenly began to fade. The fire burned his wounded hand. The earlier scar was still so fresh. Everything he had done, he had done for Garnok. Now he began to wonder: had it all been in vain? Was he expendable?

He released a tormented whimper. The power that was Garnok roared in a mimicked response.

The bigger the spectacle in the sky grew, the more his worry nervously increased. Mr. Sands hadn't felt like this for several hundred years, hadn't felt this uncertain, this scared, and this mortal, so incredibly mortal.

"Garnok?" His voice was a faint whisper in the darkness. "What's happening? What are you doing to me?"

A line of black smoke slowly rose toward his upraised hands and farther up toward his exposed throat. Mr. Sands coughed and gasped, grabbing his throat.

"It's hard to breathe," he whined, staring up at the blackish-green chaos in the sky. Pink cracks splintered across the horizon. He felt a violent pressure on his chest now. He screamed.

"Save me, Garnok! Now, I beg you! After all I've done for you, I need you to help me the way I helped you. Do you hear me?!"

The smoke curled inward, becoming denser, making its way into his eyes, nose, and mouth. The voice, rumbling and flat, came with the smoke. He hadn't heard that voice since he had made a deal many, many years ago that he had thought he would never regret.

His mortality in exchange for eternal life serving Garnok. And with that, once Garnok was liberated, a chance to once again be happy with his beloved.

Mr. Sands gasped for breath, opening his eyes. He had been anticipating happiness, ecstasy, euphoria. Certainly not this.

"I . . . I . . . I," he gasped. The smoke was suffocating him. He desperately spat and snorted. Then he heard the voice once again. It said, "Release me now! Release me, otherwise it's all over. Otherwise you're finished, John Sands."

With trembling hands, Mr. Sands started fiddling with the machine that he himself had created. His fingers didn't seem to obey him anymore. Fear had completely taken over. But he hoped that he sounded trustworthy, not scared, as he grabbed ahold of the poisonous smoke that was coiling around his neck and roared, "YOUR DELIVERANCE IS AT HAND!"

A second later, the hold on his throat eased up. The smoke rose into the air, curling through the pink cracks in the sky. Right into another world, toward the only four who still stood between Garnok and the chaos that would soon reign . . .

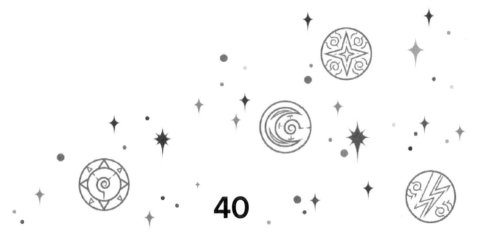

# 40

Linda continued to cling to the moon's coolness, even though she felt Sabine's breath on her face, hot and nauseating. There was something rotten and putrid about Sabine, as if she were decomposing before Linda's eyes.

At the same time, Lisa's stardust wove a sticky hold over Katja. The figure dressed in white was tossed to and fro inside the fine-meshed star web. Every time Katja moved, Lisa experienced a painful memory. Katja was somehow planting them inside her. At first, they were actual memories of things she had actually experienced. But after a while, Katja began creating false memories of terrible things that hadn't happened.

Yet.

*Watch out for the rock, Mom.*

*Blue flowers—Texas bluebells—on a dazzling white coffin.*

*Her father's sobs in an empty house, not the ranch in Texas but their house outside Jarlaheim. The guitar still hanging on the wall of her room.*

*The living room lit by the ghostly bluish light from the TV. Lisa's face filled the screen. "Lisa Peterson of Jarlaheim went out for a ride in the storm with her friends. She never came home again, leaving Carl Peterson alone in the world. All of Jorvik grieves today. Lisa was only fifteen."*

"Get out of my head, you monster!" Lisa yelled right into Katja's milk-white eyes. She yelled again and again until her own head was emptied of the nightmarish images.

Only one of the Soul Riders managed to keep out of the fray. In all the commotion, the other three had almost forgotten about her.

Alex kept a convulsive hold on Tin-Can. She tried to control the bolts of lightning whizzing out of her. She failed. A voice had bored its way into her brain and couldn't be shut out. The voice was Jessica's, honey-smooth and purring. But behind Jessica's voice there was something else booming and rumbling. Alex felt it with her whole body. How the words, if they even were words, vibrated within her like a heavy bass line.

*No one cares about you. Look for yourself. You're alone. Again. Do you really want to save them? What if you could have the whole world instead? Make people blindly obey, never have anyone push you around anymore. Wouldn't that be amazing?*

Alex trembled. The voice boomed from the rifts in the sky. A dark smoke rose up between the clouds. And a tremendous power came out of the clouds. Alex was tossed about, becoming one with the smoke and the ancient dark entity. She was pulled along in the black wave that the smoke whipped up. Maybe she was falling. Maybe she was being tossed up to extreme heights. She didn't know anymore.

The power rumbled, echoed, attracted. Muddled, Alex looked down at her palm. She saw that it was smoldering with thick, black smoke. She was the smoke. The smoke was her.

She was destruction. She was the end. She reached her hands up into the air, crying, laughing, listening.

*You have the darkness in you, Alex,* the smoke said. *Use it. It is the only way to survive. I believe that we understand each other, you and I. You don't need the others. All you need is me. I promise that you'll never need to feel lonely again, never feel misunderstood again. It will all be yours. Are you listening?*

"Yes," Alex replied in a monotone voice as she gazed up into the cracked sky. "Yes, Garnok. I hear you."

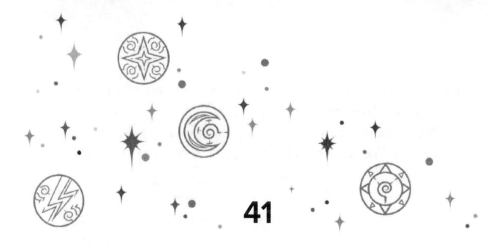

**41**

Alex raced toward the rumbling voice. The one that said she wouldn't have to feel alone anymore. That voice was all she knew at this moment. It had consumed her. She had forgotten everything else: Tin-Can and her friends, her life in Jorvik. It was all driven away by Garnok's rumbling.

"Alex, no!" the others yelled. Their voices were weak, like the quiet buzzing of a mosquito as Alex flung herself down on the ground and covered her head with her hands. She started rocking back and forth. *I am a snow globe*, she thought. *He can shake me back and forth, turn me upside down. I am nothing. But with his help, I can become everything.*

*And with your help, I will take over Jorvik*, rumbled the voice. *With your help, I will win.*

Anne threw herself at Jessica. She didn't really understand that she was the one making the animal-like noises. She just *was*. She just *did*. Sharp beams of sunlight shot out of her outstretched hand, landing on Jessica with a sizzle. Jessica screamed and scratched. Ice-cold flames rose out of her beautiful eyes. Concorde kicked backward. Wings, enormous and white as new snow, once again appeared from his sides.

"Be gone, filthy creature!" Jessica shrieked, lashing out with her arms as Concorde's wings put out her fiery flames.

Anne took the opportunity to run to her friend.

"If Garnok wins, we're nothing! We'll all die! Please don't listen, Alex!" Anne tugged on her arm. That sudden touch startled her. *"No!"* Anne yelled, continuing to pull on her. "I'm not going to let him take you. Never! Stay here with me. Can you feel me here? And feel this: here's Tin-Can, your beloved horse. He's not going to leave you. We're here." Anne pointed up at the sky and the horror that could be sensed from inside the cracks. "We'll take care of that. We'll fix this."

Alex fumbled for Tin-Can's soft coat and wished that she could believe Anne's words.

"Don't you understand?" she yelled back. "It's too late! I hear Garnok. He can do what he wants."

Anne forced Alex to look at her. She held her wet cheeks firmly between her hands.

"Don't leave us, Alex," Anne pleaded. "Stay here. We need you."

Lisa and Linda had positioned themselves with their backs together. Their fists were clenched. Jessica and Sabine stood facing them. Katja swept forward and adopted the same position. The sky roared and opened.

Garnok's words were so close that they cut into Alex, causing her whole soul to tremble.

*You can still leave them. Leave them and walk toward me. Into the darkness, into eternity. Come.*

"Come," Anne said again to Alex. "It's time now. The final battle. We can do it. Together."

*Come,* Garnok enticed. *I can offer you eternal life. You don't need anyone else, but I need you. Thousands of years in captivity. Do you understand how lonely I am? Do you understand how I have longed to escape from the shadows? Alex, you can be the chosen one. My chosen one. Come.*

An echo came out of the fog that Garnok's voice had created. Alex looked up, gazing straight into Tin-Can's eyes. His gaze was soft, but still unyielding. He looked right through her, penetrating everything that hurt and caused harm.

A bolt of lightning cut through the sky. A strange, sharp smell spread through the air, reminiscent of burned flesh.

"Is something burning?!" Lisa yelled, looking around.

Alex stood beside her, extending her singed palms up to the sky. Her face was white, her eyes wide with pain.

"Uh, I don't know exactly how that worked," Alex said doggedly. "But I think that Tin-Can and I just cut through a bit of the darkness. What if we all try doing it at the same time? The lightning, the moon, the sun, the star? And then the horses. Come on! I'm sick of listening to Garnok's nagging!"

"Yes!" Anne's voice cut through the vibrating air like a battle cry. Then she faltered and collapsed. She clutched at her neck, trying to get some air. She let out a stifled shriek. Alex bent over her friend, trying to make sure she was breathing.

But she wasn't, because a tortuous black smoke had coiled tightly around Anne's neck, constricting it like a giant snake. As Alex gasped for breath, she felt the smoke surrounding her as well. Suddenly it was hard for her to breathe, think, even move. She had been able to do all of these things just a moment before.

"Tin-Can? Under a spell?" she whispered and looked into her horse's terrified eyes. He brayed. Yet another poisonous plume of smoke wreathed around, settling like a noose around Tin-Can's frantically snorting muzzle. His hooves moved, but he couldn't get anywhere.

And Alex felt the lightning bolts desert her, one by one.

Sabine stood beside her, laughing.

Then something slipped through Sabine's mocking laughter, something velvety soft. All of Pandoria was filled with song. Lisa was singing, and in time with her tune, little star-shaped spirals rose up into the sky. She sang to Anne, who was having trouble breathing. She sang to Alex who was trying to reach her terrified horse. The song turned into swirling stars that shot off toward Anne's throat. Her eyes were bulging so much in fear that Lisa was afraid they would pop out of her head. Lisa's voice trembled. Her whole body shook, but she sang, and she sang. Behind her, an ancient sound rose from Starshine.

Next to Alex, a meteorite traveled through the vibrating, sickly pink air. And Linda and Meteor followed it.

Two of the Soul Riders and two of the horses were still free. They would free the others now.

If it was the last thing they did.

Suddenly Sabine, Jessica, and Katja were flung into the air by a massive shock wave, causing their eardrums to vibrate. They traveled like projectiles until they disappeared right into the cracks in the ground. Their roaring shook all of Pandoria. The Soul Riders' light spirals chased after the Dark Riders, trying to close the cracks.

Then they were gone.

"Three down," Alex said, wiping her palms on her pants. "One massive super-evil bad guy to go."

Alex laughed in relief, but her laugh froze in her throat. Her body started shaking when she saw the smoke coiling through the rifts like starving boa constrictors, headed straight for Linda and Meteor. Linda gasped for breath, grasping at her throat with her hands. She couldn't get any air. She was sure she was suffocating. She desperately tried to get some air down her constricted throat.

Alex screamed when she saw the black cloud of smoke coming out of Linda's eyes.

"Linda, no! Don't let him take you! He can't have you, Linda!"

It was like being consumed by an infinite darkness. When you are consumed by a darkness like that, you quickly forget who you are. Linda opened her eyes and listened.

*Take the step.* The voice was like slippery stones in an icy October ocean. *Just one little step and then you're with us. You'll never need to be afraid again.*

The ground shook. A shimmering green crack formed underneath them. Linda tripped. The voice continued to chant, speaking to her alone. *Imagine how wonderful it would be never to be afraid again, never to need anything at all, to be free of everything, no more fear or anxiety, no doubt. You're safe with us, Linda.*

The black smoke brought tears to Linda's eyes. She coughed, wheezed, spat out shiny black saliva that landed on the ground with a sizzle.

Then she felt it: a warm hand propping her up, another voice, Alex's voice, cracked and hoarse.

"Linda, don't listen," Alex urged. "We're here."

Another voice said, "Yes, we're here."

A third, "We're here, Linda."

Now she could hear Lisa singing again. She had probably never stopped singing. Lisa's song floated over Garnok's slippery calls. Linda focused on the song, on the hand squeezing her shoulder.

"It's working," Alex whispered, her breath warm on Linda's ear. "You can feel it, too, can't you?"

"Now I can," Linda replied, watching as their magic rose from them, all at the same time now.

The sun. The lightning. The star. The symbols swirled in the air, coiling together and forming a beautiful, elegant pattern on the tattered canvas of the heavens. And now the moon was visible, too. Linda gasped when she saw that her outstretched hand was silvery-white with moonlight. She felt the moonlight pulsating through her, growing stronger along with Lisa's song.

The sky turned inside out, becoming a brilliant white. The cracks could still be made out, thin, green veins in the ground surrounding them. A voice hissed at them through time and space. They recognized the voice. It said, *"You'll regret this. You don't know the powers you're playing with. This isn't over."*

The storm swirled, whipping up a cloud of pink dust. Sabine's horse, Khaan, stepped out of this dust. Through the rifts, they could hear Sabine's triumphant voice.

"It's not over until I say it is!" she bellowed. "Get her, Khaan!"

A tremendous roar was followed by the ground shaking with thundering hooves. Khaan raced toward Linda. His big, muscular body was covered with scars. Linda tried to move but couldn't get anywhere. She was knocked over, crawling backward. Soon she would be crushed by those enormous hooves coming towards her . . .

Meteor made an ear-deafening shriek, reared up, and began galloping straight toward Khaan. Starshine, Tin-Can, and Concorde followed him at the same furious pace. They drove Khaan away from Linda, pushing, blocking, feinting. A whooshing, swishing noise filled the air as large, dazzlingly white wings emerged from the horses' backs. Not just Concorde, but all four of them. Linda stood transfixed, staring.

The wings whipped at Khaan. The enormous black horse bellowed, more monster than horse now. He rose up onto his hind legs and staggered backward.

The moonlight soared up through the silvery threads. Alex gasped, seeing the light and the horses pushing Khaan backward, deeper and deeper into the crack. Khaan was pushed even farther in by a new, powerful shock wave and then completely disappeared. A deep growl pressed through all the narrow rifts. It echoed across the sky, which now pulsed with fireworks of colors—white, black, pink, and green. The colors formed a colorful pattern of stars, lightning bolts, suns, and moons.

The heat that spread between the four was almost unbearable, but they directed it away from themselves, down at the ground where Garnok's poisonous smoke continued to spread. They coughed, their eyes full of tears. The dizziness made their legs give way. They felt the horses' presence intensely. Their wings spread out behind them as protection. Under the horses' wings, they were strong. They realized they were no longer afraid.

Could their light become so strong that it would burn through the darkness? That was exactly what they were planning to try.

Using the light that they created together, they shot at Garnok again and again. That nasty, burnt smell returned. The air crackled with electricity.

"Look!" Linda yelled. Her face was shiny with sweat, her whole body trembled, and she could feel how manic her smile was. She saw the same smile appear on the others' faces.

Where Garnok's presence had clung a moment before, cracks had now formed again—and now the black smoke was being squeezed back into the cracks. One last, ear-splitting roar shook Pandoria. When the darkness fled, the sky turned a luminescent white.

And then everything was quiet.

They stood together, hand in hand, for a long time. They watched the dazzling white sky slowly saturate with pink hues.

Dusk fell over Pandoria in deep pink shadows. The air was almost wintery cold against their hot cheeks.

"I'll take us home now," Anne said.

And then, as they all held hands, she did.

It was evening in Jorvik as the last Soul Riders returned to our world. In a small house on the outskirts of Jarlaheim, a man heard a deafening explosion and raced out the front door. Could that have been a lightning strike? *Yikes, that only barely missed the house,* Carl Peterson thought, shaking his head.

Then he paused, right by the old apple tree, and squinted at the light in the sky. He looked at the sun's rays, which suddenly, inexplicably, warmed his cheeks. Surprised, he lifted his hands into the air. The storm had subsided. The evening sunlight bathed the whole yard in a golden glow. The light danced and finally landed on the heaps of apples lying in drifts on the ground. When his daughter came home again, they should pick up the apples, he thought. Maybe they could make a pie out of the apples that were still in good shape. He thought about how much he'd enjoy being with his daughter in their cozy little kitchen, chatting about nothing in particular. Not about evil or dark corners, but about completely normal things—the stables, some silly TV show, a memory they shared, life.

He stood quietly in the light of the setting sun and smiled. And then, even though he knew no one could hear him, he whispered: "Isa, I knew you could do it."

## 42

A few weeks later, Lisa turned around in her saddle and called back over her shoulder to her friends.

"Come on, let's gallop!"

The woods opened up around them and the sun sparkled through the treetops. The hint of frost on the pine needles covering the forest floor and the dry brown leaves whispered that winter would soon be here. Above the firs, the sky was unbelievably blue for as far as you could see.

They broke into a gallop and became one with their horses' smooth, undulating motions. As the trail narrowed, they slowed down and walked for a while. Linda brought her horse over close to Lisa and sighed happily. Her eyeglasses were completely fogged up.

"Can you believe we're actually here now?" she said, giving her horse the reins. "We just rode in the woods as if nothing ever happened. We did it!"

"It's already starting to feel like something that happened to someone else," Lisa said, caressing Starshine's silky white neck with a thoughtful look in her eyes, "like in some crazy movie or something, even though it *actually* did happen to us."

They had ridden into a little sun-drenched clearing where they walked along side by side. The mountains were discernable in the distance, tall and blue in the late afternoon light. Lisa looked at the peaks and wondered if those were the same mountains she had seen when she and her father had driven off the car ferry that early September morning, their first morning in Jorvik. It felt like so long ago now. Almost like another lifetime.

She looked around at the horses and their riders. Reliable Meteor with his wide, white blaze and those wise eyes. Graceful Concorde with his neatly groomed mane and dreamlike motions. Even now as they walked in the woods, the back of his gray, shiny neck was bent elegantly. He practically danced along in the soft light. Next to him, Tin-Can pretty much looked like a disobedient little pony. His thick brown coat was already starting to look a bit shaggy, like a winter coat. His small ears were pricked forward. His eyes were alert and mischievous.

Each horse paired perfectly with his rider in his own, unique way. Lisa's heart felt light and warm as she thought about how happy she was that she had come to Jorvik. She had friends for life here. The girls riding with her today were her sisters, today and always.

A crow cawed and flew deeper into the woods. Lisa glanced at the dark shadows that had spread through the woods beyond the clearing. She didn't want to go in there, not today. She wanted to ride in the sunshine now with her Soul Rider sisters and not think about what was hiding in the darkness.

She knew all too well how easily one could end up there.

With Lisa in the lead, they turned around and started walking back toward the stables in restful silence. The air was fresh and crisp to breathe.

"And now what?" Anne gave voice to what they were all thinking. "What happens now?"

"With us or with Jorvik?" Alex wondered.

"How about both?" Anne smiled.

"Yeah, what happens now?" Linda repeated. "Does your dad still want you guys to move?"

"He's actually been really quiet on that front," Lisa said, grinning when her words were met with a cheer. "Plus, one other thing. I received an acceptance letter in the mail today," Lisa admitted. The corners of her mouth twitched with pride.

"From the music school?!" Anne and Linda exclaimed in unison. "No way! That's so great!"

"I knew it!" Alex said. Her eyes were warm below her unruly, light-brown bangs. "When do you start?"

"Right after Christmas break," Lisa responded.

Alex leaned back in her saddle and looked up at the sky.

"It still feels like we're going to drift apart," Alex finally said. "That always happens. People promise they'll always be friends and then everything gets in the way. Life gets in the way. Who's to say that we'll be any different?"

"No way!" Lisa responded emphatically. "Just because we're not all going to the same school, that doesn't have to mean that we'll stop hanging out. The fact is," she added, her eyes twinkling, "that I simply won't allow that. You can just forget about that. The three of you are the best friends I've ever had, the *only* friends I've ever had, if we're being specific. I'm planning to spam call you guys all the time about getting together for movie nights and going out riding! And when it comes time for me to perform at music school, I'm going to *require* you guys to come and to sit in the very front and cheer me on!"

"You know we will." Alex smiled. Linda and Anne nodded in agreement. Tin-Can craned his neck and snorted.

"What about all the other stuff?" Anne asked hesitantly. "Do we have that under control?"

"If by *all the other stuff* you mean the whole Soul Rider thing, I talked to Herman and Elizabeth," Alex replied. "I'm going to keep helping the druids. Elizabeth and I decided that. I'll keep an eye on the flow of energy so that nothing gets out of control. It should be calm for now, but it's best to be certain." She patted her chest. "I'll wear the sheriff's badge while the rest of you take over the world. That makes the most sense since you guys are all going off to other places."

"I'm not planning on going anywhere," Linda reassured her. "I said that already, right?"

"Well, not *now*, no," Alex said. Her eyes seemed several shades darker, even in the sparkling sunlight. "But later on. I'm sure you'll get into some amazing university somewhere and Lisa will become a rock star and Anne will be the dressage world champion. And I'll stay here and make sure that Jorvik remains safe. I mean, someone has to do it, and I don't mind."

The instant she said that out loud, she realized it was true. There was something nice about being the one who stayed put. And there was nowhere else she'd rather be than at Jorvik Stables.

And if there was, it would probably be the Secret Stone Circle anyway. Since they had returned home from Pandoria, Alex had been spending a lot of time with Elizabeth and the druids. With each new thing she learned, she felt that much more confident that she was doing the right thing by sticking to magic while the others tried to resume their everyday lives.

Because it wasn't possible to give up the magic entirely. They were still Soul Riders after all, and Fripp had already said that a time would come when they would need to be ready once again. In the meantime, there was Alex.

"I'm glad it's you," Lisa said in a warm voice. "Jorvik is in safe hands as long as you're still here."

"Really," Anne agreed. "I can't think of anyone better."

"Me either," Linda said.

"Come on, let's gallop!" Alex called out. When no one was looking she wiped a tear from the corner of her eye.

And as they galloped away, the wind played in their hair. Butterflies filled their stomachs as the horses sped up, almost flying.

"It smells like snow, you know?" Lisa yelled.

"How many times do I need to tell you that snow doesn't have a smell?" Alex yelled back, annoyed.

"And songs have no color . . . well, aside from Lisa's songs, that is." Linda grinned.

"Of course," Anne agreed. She was breathless from the fast ride and excessive grinning.

This moment together would always be theirs. Maybe the memory would fade over time, like the colors in an old photograph. Maybe other moments in the future would replace this specific one. Shared moments, and times when they were apart. Times of joy, times of sorrow, triumph, and fear.

There was so much left. The Soul Riders' story was still written here and in the stars.

Fripp was standing at his lookout place up at the Secret Stone Circle just then, contemplating what was to come.

Far beyond the chilly Jorvegian woods, Garnok writhed in his captivity.

In a darkened room at Pine Hill Mansion, John Sands stared blankly out in front of him. He was surrounded by ripped-up diary entries and scorched maps. His already ravaged face looked aged, despondent. With a frustrated growl, he threw his shredded diaries away, pulled out a fresh, new book, and began to write.

There was so much that hadn't happened yet.

But now the autumn's first snow began to fall softly from the sky. Lisa noticed it first and squealed in delight. The snowflakes continued to fall on Starshine's blue mane until it appeared totally white. They galloped faster. Someone yelled: "Last one back to the stables is a rotten egg!" And then the race was on. Flushed cheeks. Breathing hard. Cheerful horses with their ears pricked. Happy laughter echoed through the air. There was a sweet smell, almost vaguely metallic, the way it always smelled when the very first snow fell.

They shared this moment together, for a little while longer. And right now, at this moment, that was what mattered most.

# Epilogue

And so, we leave the beautiful island of Jorvik—a place that contains great evil, but also boundless courage. The Soul Riders' sisterhood has risen up and the dark forces seem, at least for the moment, to have been defeated.

But Garnok continues fighting to get free. True evil needs to be patient. It must bide its time, must not be overly hasty.

At the same time, evil is by nature unrestrained. We see that everywhere—not just in Jorvik. How evil begets evil, how clueless-ness allows it to thrive. It is so tempting to avert one's gaze, pretend not to notice. But that's just what the evil wants. The power that wants to harm Jorvik and the Soul Riders will strike again. No one knows if it will happen tomorrow or in forty years. Not even Fripp can read this in the stars.

But one thing is clear. When the time comes, when doubts grow, and the darkness again falls over Jorvik—they will be ready once again.

Four completely normal, extraordinary girls, with completely normal, extraordinary dreams, wishes, and fears, just like you.

They are the last sisterhood, and by Aideen's Light: they intend to never give up. They plan to go on shining, twinkling, sparkling, and burning. Like the first girl on horseback who brought life to Jorvik with her light, their passion is infinite, even though they don't always realize it themselves. Maybe they're not meant to, either. How else could they manage to live their everyday lives?

But the passion, love, and power are there. And so is the hope. And as long as they have each other and their horses, nothing, not even evil itself, can stop them.

# Acknowledgments

You've surely heard the expression "It takes a village to raise a child"? Writing a trilogy of books requires, if not a whole village, then at any rate a small army of cheerleaders and sharp-eyed people. I want to thank some of them here:

Team Bonnier Carlsen, especially Anton Klepke and Ulrika Caperius. You were true workhorses! Marcus Olsson for the encouragement and clever solutions. Marcus Thorell Björkäng for making sure that I didn't get lost in Jorvik. Marie Beschorner for the delightful covers. All of Star Stable's amazing game masters and social media profiles that spread so much joy. Niklas Wennergren for all you do for my books at the local level. Librarians and booksellers for safeguarding literature. My mother and father for always being willing to help. Marcus Stenberg for teaching me to operate a wood stove, ride a scooter, and stand up for myself even though it's the scariest thing in the world. And for giving me the most wonderful thing an author can have: a room of one's own. All my wonderful author friends for being on-call on Messenger and for sharing wine and friendship with me. My children for putting up with a mother whose head is always up in the clouds. I love you to the moon and back!

Finally, a thank you to everyone who reads and writes. Stories, aren't they great?! I believe stories are what hold us together, now more than ever. So, I raise my cold coffee and drink a toast to stories. May we read them, and may we continue to write them.

—Helena Dahlgren, January 2020

First published by Bonnier Carlsen Bokförlag, Stockholm, Sweden.
Published in the English language by agreement with Ferly.

Andrews McMeel Publishing
a division of Andrews McMeel Universal
1130 Walnut Street, Kansas City, Missouri 64106

www.andrewsmcmeel.com

21 22 23 24 25 RR4 10 9 8 7 6 5 4 3 2 1

Paperback ISBN: 978-1-5248-5620-5
Hardback ISBN: 978-1-5248-5971-8

Library of Congress Control Number: 2020951992

Made by:
LSC Communications US, LLC
Address and location of manufacturer:
2347 Kratzer Road
Harrisonburg, VA 22802
1st Printing – 2/15/21

Writer: Helena Dahlgren
Synopsis and concept development: Marcus Thorell Björkäng
Language editors: Anton Klepke and Marcus Thorell Björkäng
Editor: Jean Z. Lucas
Cover design: Malin Gustavsson
Cover art: Marie Beschorner
Art Director: Spencer Williams
Production Manager: Chuck Harper
Production Editor: David Shaw

ATTENTION: SCHOOLS AND BUSINESSES
Andrews McMeel books are available at quantity discounts with bulk purchase for educational, business, or sales promotional use. For information, please e-mail the Andrews McMeel Publishing Special Sales Department: specialsales@amuniversal.com.